The Waiter

The Waiter

Matias Faldbakken

Translated from the Norwegian by Alice Menzies

Doubleday

LONDON · TORONTO · SYDNEY · AUCKLAND · JOHANNESBURG

TRANSWORLD PUBLISHERS
61–63 Uxbridge Road, London W5 5SA
www.penguin.co.uk

Transworld is part of the Penguin Random House group of companies
whose addresses can be found at global.penguinrandomhouse.com

First published in Great Britain in 2018 by Doubleday
an imprint of Transworld Publishers
Published by agreement with Salomonsson Agency

This translation has been published with the financial support of NORLA.

The lyrics on p. 95 are taken from 'Gli Impermeabili' written by Paolo Conte.

A CIP catalogue record for this book
is available from the British Library.

ISBN 9780857525857

Typeset in 11/15 pt Minion Pro by Jouve (UK), Milton Keynes
Printed and bound in Great Britain by Clays Ltd, Elcograf S.p.A.

Penguin Random House is committed to a sustainable
future for our business, our readers and our planet. This book
is made from Forest Stewardship Council® certified paper.

1 3 5 7 9 10 8 6 4 2

To Ida

A scared dog never gets fat.
(Norwegian proverb)

PART I

The Pig

The Hills dates from a time when pigs were pigs and swine were swine. Or so the Maître D' likes to say. In other words, from the mid nineteenth century. And here I stand, straight-backed in my waiter's uniform, just as I might have done a hundred years ago or more. People do extreme things every day. But not me. No. I wait. I aim to please. I move around the room taking orders, pouring drinks and clearing away. At The Hills, people can gorge themselves in surroundings that are rich in tradition. They should feel welcome, but not so comfortable that they forget where they are. There are a few notable exceptions; some of the diners use the place like their own parlour.

Apropos pigs: one of our regulars, The Pig (Mr Graham went grey during his twenties while he was pursuing his career in Paris, and was nicknamed *Le Gris*, which immediately became *Grisen* – The Pig – on his return to Norway) sits by the window at table 10 from half past one every weekday.

He tends to be punctual, but it's now 13.41 and he hasn't made an appearance. I do a loop of the entrance: no Pig. The cloak-room attendant, Pedersen, glances up from his paper. Pedersen is distinguished-looking, as they say. It seems he's seen it all. The guests trade their possessions – jackets, coats, bags, umbrellas – for a tag which they later, accompanied by a coin or two, swap back for the same possessions when they leave. He has carried out these transactions with com-posure and pride all these years; he does his job well. We're all diligent here at The Hills. It's a diligent place. Diligence and anxiety go hand in hand, I'm convinced of that.

Lunch is under way, and the main room has filled up with the upper-middle class: silky-skinned, softly spoken, elegantly clothed. There is a row of smaller café tables with classic marble tops by the entrance. There, the acoustics are sharper. Deeper into the room, tablecloths have been draped over the tables. There is clinking, but the noise is muted. Cutlery is moved around porcelain and up to mouths. Teeth chew, throats rise, fall and swallow. It's all about eating in here, and I'm a facilitator. I never take part in the eating myself, rather I observe the consumption. There's a considerable distance between the experience of ingesting a strong Picodon goat's cheese – the gastronomic explosion in one's mouth – and watching the lips of some-one else doing it. I set the tables as densely as possible, continental style. There's not quite enough room, but I find space and squeeze in extra glasses, side plates, another bottle. It all feels rich and full.

The chandelier isn't especially big, no bigger than a

horse's nosebag, but it is heavy, and hangs like a crystal sack from the low vaulted ceiling above the round table in the middle of the room. Lining the floor are concentric circles of well-trampled mosaic tiles. All the woodwork is solid, dark and worn. The two large mirrors are impressive. The reflective coating on the back of the glass has cracked here and there. It lends a nice patina. The art nouveau-esque oak frames around the mirrors were added in 1901. Or so the Bar Manager told me, elaborating with details about how the wood was dragged down from Ekeberg by the landscape painter Frits Thaulow's very own horse. The Bar Manager is the restaurant's memory; her face looks learned like an academic's, but she's a bit too cheerful to be an academic. She sees everything.

The Hills might resemble a Viennese coffee house, but this isn't Vienna. It may look like an institution in keeping with the *Grand European* tradition, but it's too worn, too grimy to match the grandeur you would find on the continent. The establishment, the premises, has been called The Hills for almost 150 years now. The name comes from the Hill family, who ran an outfitter's shop here from 1846. The Bar Manager knows all about that. Benjamin Hill, the scion of the family, was a legendary but tragic dandy, originally from Windsor in England, who gambled away two-thirds of the family fortune and stumbled into a painful bankruptcy; after a failed suicide attempt, he lived out the rest of his days as an invalid. The entrepreneur who took over the space opened a restaurant called La Grenade, but the original stained-glass sign covering parts of the façade was so lavish and elaborate, not to mention well mounted, that he left it there, and the place became known popularly as The Hills. Benjamin Hill's energetic son eventually bought back the premises, took over the business and resurrected the family name. The Hills remains under family control to this day.

From a curved brass rod installed above the entrance hang two thick drapes – to keep the heat in – each with calfskin sewn on to the edge to prevent wear and tear. In through this stage curtain, if you like, enters The Pig at last, smiling and nodding. It's almost ten to two, just about tolerable. I neither nod nor smile back. I'm fundamentally neither a smiler nor a nodder. It's a blank but obliging face I assume for the guests. A poker face is all part of the craft.

'Sorry I'm late,' The Pig says, laughing apologetically, not with a grunt but with some kind of neigh.

'How many today?'

'Four, myself included.'

'And the others are on their way?'

'I expect so.'

There are many ways to dress, but The Pig has chosen the only acceptable one: impeccably. He constantly has new suits, and judging by the cut, the stitching and the quality of the fabric, they must be from tailors on Savile Row or thereabouts. He keeps his thick, greyish-white hair short with a weekly trim. His eyebrows are still dark, giving him an intelligent look, like Leo Castelli, or a canine air, like Scorsese. With an age of just over three-score years, and dressed in such a wardrobe on a daily basis, he is in every sense an elegant man and a model guest. The Pig fits The Hills like a glove. That's why we give him some leeway with the number of guests, late arrivals, fussing over the table, and so on. Not that it happens often. The Pig is wealthy, that much is clear, but he is also some kind of introvert. Steadily, quietly, he brings new contacts and acquaintances to The Hills, primarily for lunch, occasionally for dinner, always polite and always with his impeccable attire and manners.

'We've held the usual window table for you,' I say, holding out my hand as I take four menus and lead him through the room. With perfect timing, I pull out his chair and repeat the set phrase: 'Some mineral water while you wait?'

'Yes, please.'

He turns around and allows me to gently push the chair into the hollows of his knees.

Blaise

Old Johansen, the house pianist, is sitting at the grand piano on the mezzanine, looking at the vaulted ceiling or, to his left, into thin air. His stubby, pope-like fingers dance over the keys with a light touch and considerable experience, producing seamless, barely audible music. Is this muzak? He chooses the great composers, Johansen does, but it's still muzak. Occasionally, his eyes close as the notes trill in all directions, down into the restaurant. Old, stuffed-shirt Johansen. His head droops, and it looks like he's nodded off for a moment, but then it rolls back into position and his eyes snap open. He carries on like that for hours. For a generation and a half now, he's been there, for endless stretches at a time, his head bobbing away, every day, on the mezzanine, that mid-ceiling, playing pleasant tunes in succession for the guests. Since we arrive at different times, we rarely speak, but people say he has a sharp sense of humour.

The neatly folded napkins are stacked on a low shelf between two pillars in the middle of the room. A glass screen with pale art nouveau lines stands on top of the shelf, acting as a buffer between tables 12 and 8. If I find myself empty-handed, I often go over to that shelf, where I stand behind the screen and straighten the napkins with an extra crease. The new girl, Vanessa, is a bit careless in this respect. I make sure that the Hills logo is in the top right-hand corner.

'Do you have the white burgundy today?' says The Pig.

'Of course.'

I wait two tasteful beats before I ask the next question, to which I already know the answer.

'By the glass? Or are we having a bottle?'

The Pig considers this.

'Listen, let's have a bottle.'

He suddenly gets up – I barely manage to pull out the chair for him in time. He extends his hands to a handsome couple approaching between the tables.

'Blaise!' The Pig says enthusiastically, pronouncing the name as 'Blez!'. And then, affectionately: 'Katharina.'

Blaise Engelbert is Katharina's husband, Katharina is Blaise's wife. They socialize with The Pig quite often, particularly Blaise. Blaise and his wife have married the mature versions of one another, the Bar Manager likes to say ('the old version' being a little unkind, she qualifies). After their respective detours around Oslo society, they found one another, and are now, the Bar Manager further informs me, the oldest person the other has ever been with.

Katharina is in front, and puts one foot before the other in such a way that her well-maintained mid-forties figure is propelled with determination in the direction of The Pig. Right behind her is Blaise, some seven years older, wearing a grey suit with attractive stitching on a par with The Pig's, possibly even a notch superior. Blaise has an excellent tie around his neck and a spring in his step. 'Finesse' is the word that always hangs in the air around this man. I tiptoe in their wake, and pull out their chairs as they confirm that they would both like water and wine.

The menu looks French and is delicately typeset in a softly spaced Bodoni. These are some of the words that appear on its two densely printed pages: crackling, plaice, kid, blue cheese, cumin, profiteroles, Jerusalem artichoke, tart, bouillabaisse, squid, vendace roe, dates, brisket, rillettes and minke. To all this and more, the customers can point and have it prepared – with knowledge and flair – by the Chef and his assistants. In due course I (or Vanessa, for example) bring out the dishes, which they then raise to their mouths bit by bit. Truffles are also available. The truffle is key.

Vanessa, the new waitress with a gentle face, a short, boyish hairstyle, and a talent hampered by ambition, straightens the tablecloths while I do a lap of the room, topping up a glass here and being pleasant to somebody else there. The poor actor who was recently convicted of fraud gets a refill; he's already starting to go slack-eyed. After The Pig's companions have looked at the menu for a minute or two, I'm there pouring them water. Blaise brusquely rejects the white burgundy before I even have time to ask. He takes several large gulps of water, and I immediately refill his glass. Then he gives the sign that I can pour the wine. I turn the bottle clockwise after each pour, to catch the last drop. Tactfully, I lean over The Pig's shoulder and gently ask whether we are waiting for a fourth and final person. The Pig looks at his watch.

'Has anyone heard from her? It's three minutes past two. She's over half an hour late.'

Blaise and his wife shake their heads.

'She did confirm?' Blaise says.

'Of course,' says The Pig. 'Absolutely.'

The back of Blaise's head is oblong and youthful. He cranes his neck and peers towards the entrance. His hairline is classic and clean and complements his jawline. The angle of his nose and brow, and the curve of his cheekbones, are also repeated with pleasing symmetry by his hairline, as it runs from his temple down to his ear. His neck is boyish, despite his age, his eyes alert. The collar of his shirt sits a comfortable six to seven millimetres away from the skin of his neck, in a beautiful fold. Blaise is fit, but it's not overdone; he's sharp, but not severe. Katharina and The Pig lean forward when he speaks, almost in a whisper. Blaise's voice is unusual. Where you might expect a bombastic tone, like so often with handsome, almost pompous men, he produces a firm, authoritative, but friendly – even verging on sensual – voice.

'Would you like to wait a while longer?' I say, not a trace of pushiness in my voice.

The Pig checks the time again, as Blaise raises his left arm to shake out his watch. It turns out to be an impressive A. Lange & Söhne. It couldn't be a Grand Lange I, could it? There's a hint of braggadocio in him.

'You can take our orders now, and the latecomer can . . .' The Pig says, gesturing, first with one hand and then with the other, that the latecomer can order when she arrives.

I turn my attention to Blaise's wife to indicate that she can begin. Katharina chooses a mixed salad with Monte Enebro goat's cheese, nuts, seeds and passion fruit vinaigrette.

'Could I have extra nuts and seeds?' she asks.

'Extra nuts and seeds,' I say.

Blaise changes his mind twice before he plumps for the creamy orzo with shallots. It's obvious that his indecision grates slightly with The Pig – obvious to me, not the Engelberts. I turn to The Pig. It's his turn. He takes his time.

'The brown Valdres trout,' he says.

'Yes?'

'What kind of crispbread comes with it?'

'We have a crispbread from Hemsedal.'

'Right.'

'We have a wonderful soured cream dip to go with it,' I say, with a hooked index finger pointing downwards to illustrate 'dip'. What am I doing?

'Thanks, but no. No dip for me. I'll try the trout.'

'Wonderful.'

The Walls

A long the wainscoting, which runs beneath all of the portraits, drawings and paintings here at The Hills, a number of stickers have been put up over the years. We allow it. That's the way it's always been. The practice has died down somewhat now, but the odd new sticker still appears from time to time. It's not clear how it all began, but there are rumours that some 'avant-gardists' who frequented the place during the 1920s did it to play a prank on a rich man who had a regular table at the other end of the room. What these jokes consisted of is difficult to see through today's optics, but down by the skirting board there are old, yellowed fragments of press cuttings about this financier, Mr Grosch. The avant-gardists cut out thin columns from the newspapers and glued them to the wall, often horizontally, at the very bottom; these were gestures directed at Mr Grosch, gestures of spite.

The crude clippings later crept upwards from the

skirting board and were followed during the '30s and '40s by flyers and small pamphlets, manifestos – primarily political material – before being covered over by advertising stickers during the '60s and '70s: old STP and Gulf images to begin with, then Castrol and RFI, followed by football teams and rowing clubs and so on, resulting in the composite that now covers the wainscoting. If you took a cross-section of the panelling, you could carry out an archaeological study of it, from early bohemian life to sport and commerce; from the oldest, crustiest layers, which are golden brown and look almost like parchment, to the outer, fresher stickers. The wainscoting itself, small glimpses of which can be seen between the layers, is dark and matte, nearly as black as the ceiling above the range in the kitchen. It's difficult to see where the stickers end and the wainscoting begins – indeed, where The Hills begins or ends, depending on whether you consider a wall to be the beginning or the end of a room, a locale, an establishment. Europe has certainly seen better days. One could claim that Europe's best ever idea was the *Grand European*.

Above the wainscoting, paintings, drawings and the odd collage are crammed tightly together on the – and I apologize for this – diarrhoea-brown walls, with their coat upon coat of shiny beige paint. Or is it lacquer? The art has 'accumulated' over the years, meaning that it's impossible to describe The Hills' collection as anything other than considerable in a national context. There's a Revold hanging on one wall, a Per Krohg, and even a small Oda Krohg sketch by table 5. Back in the 1990s, there was a lot of talk about conservation and the conditions inside The Hills, but the family has always taken a hard line, insisting that the pictures donated to the restaurant should remain there. It's easier now, after the smoking ban, but some of the older material is fairly snuff-coloured.

A small, pre-Cubist Braque landscape in oils hangs above table 6, believe it or not. There's also a first-rate Léger in chalk by the screen. The simple Schwitters collage framed in hideous teak to the right, above the bar, was donated by Schwitters himself when he was en route from Hjertøya to the capital in '34 or '35. Gunnar S. has two handsome prints at one end of the room, plus one beneath the mezzanine. Large and small works are hung side by side, all mixed up. There has never been any talk of 're-hanging' the pictures here at The Hills. They simply hang *more*. Contemporary art is squeezed into the gaps between older works. It's old and new, clean and grimy, side by side. The quality varies considerably. A fifteen-by-twenty-centimetre charcoal sketch from the hand of Anders Svor hangs frame to frame with an early Polaroid by Ed Ruscha. A Finn Graff caricature of Vladimir Putin as a lemur touches, physically, a Kippenberger postcard of middling quality. It's like that up and down the walls, from top to bottom, right down to the wainscoting where the stickers begin. Yes, I said a Kippenberger. We also have a garish but good little Shearer of a metalhead standing on a ridge, gazing over the mountains.

*

It's in relation to The Hills' art collection that another of the regulars, Tom Sellers, comes into the picture. Tom Sellers is the polar opposite of The Pig. Sellers was in Düsseldorf and Cologne (the right place at the right time) and became a figure on the scene around Kippenberger, so they say. Sellers has always denied it; such Kippenberger connections are double-edged swords. Sellers has never been an artist himself, he's not interested. But like everyone who was a 'figure' on the 'scene' 'around Kippenberger', he carries a hint of that aura, and he certainly knows several of the other 'figures' from the scene – meaning he also has access to this piece or that, which most people do not. A good number of the best works donated over the past fifteen to twenty years are hanging here thanks to Tom Sellers. It was he who gave us the simple little Werner Tübke drawing of a foot, which hangs above one end of the bar. His crowning glory is the tiny Victor Hugo watercolour of an octopus above a castle in the Rhine Valley, made using soot, coffee and coal dust. Through his donations, Sellers has built up a considerable amount of goodwill here. His contributions, however, come with an appendage, a protuberance, an *avec* – a pendant of slacking, disorder and unruliness. But there's a place for that at The Hills, too. We should be tolerant here, says M. Hill, the General Manager. I agree. Some days, though, I don't.

There are also portraits of past regulars on the walls. In addition to being a personality (in finance, culture, academia), you have to spend both time and a pretty penny here. The actor (blown, bankrupt) hasn't qualified for a

16

portrait, and considering the fine he was handed down after the fraud scandal, the question remains as to how much he'll be able to spend in the future. A portrait of The Pig is also conspicuous by its absence, but for other reasons; The Pig offered a polite 'no' when the General Manager suggested it may be time for a portrait. The Pig has good taste. He's certainly interested in art. Rumour has it he has a wonderful Kittelsen at home. 'You know,' The Pig said to M. Hill (according to the Bar Manager), 'when you've studied Carl Larsson's etchings like I have all these years, well, it's a bit tricky to find a portrait artist who ... well, you understand. You know ... now, today. But, thank you.'

Young Lady

The latecomer still hasn't arrived when I serve The Pig his food.

'Would you be so kind as to check whether our friend has made an appearance in the cloakroom? A young girl . . . lady,' he says quietly.

'Certainly,' I say.

The Pig pulls out his phone and shows me a picture of the girl. What kind of tasteless behaviour is this? Very unlike The Pig. There's a small queue by the cloakroom. They're all older, and men. I don't really know who I'm looking for, but since 'young' and 'girl . . . lady' is the description, it doesn't look good. Old Pedersen is handling nothing but men's jackets, one after the other.

'Is there anyone here to meet Mr Graham?' I ask. Four of them don't react, and one shakes his head. I ask Pedersen, but he hasn't seen anyone like that. I go out on to the street and look towards the tram stop, then downhill in the direction of Parliament. My eyes move over the so-called 'dance hole', a small dip in the ground where Widow Knipschild once tripped. She stumbled and had to take long steps to stop herself falling, swinging her arms from side to side in some kind of razzle-dazzle, hence the name dance hole; all the waiting staff saw it. It's late November, and though it's a glorious day, I can't quite take it in. Habit is like a blanket which settles over the nature of things. The city is colourless, despite the brilliant autumn sun. Always the same, banal.

'I couldn't find her.'

'Hmm.'

The Pig allows himself a slow sip of white burgundy. Blaise's eyes are fixed on him.

'Let me know if there's anything else,' I say.

In the nineteen years I've worked here, I've never seen anyone be short-tempered or unpleasant in The Pig's company, but Blaise is speaking to The Pig in a firm tone now.

And The Pig, who couldn't by any means be described as yielding or weak, is making a series of apologetic gestures. Eventually, at 14.22, Blaise stands up so abruptly that his chair toots against the floor; he throws down his linen napkin and walks towards the exit with stiff, businesslike steps. I glance at the Bar Manager to make sure she has seen it – she has, of course – before I move forward and cross a line by placing my hand between the shoulder blades of a slightly flustered Pig. Katharina is still sitting, stabbing at the nuts and seeds, before she mechanically puts her things back into her handbag and silently gets up.

'Is everything OK here?'

'Indeed,' says The Pig.

'Would you like anything else?'

'No, thank you. I'll have the bill.'

The Pig plucks at his wad of banknotes and Vanessa clears the table, slightly too soon, slightly too hectically. None of the three has finished their meal, and the white burgundy will have to be poured away; the bottle is still half full of golden drops. I'll do that job, I'm happy to pour white burgundy down the drain. Grape juice from Aloxe-Corton vanishes into the sewer. The Pig remains in his seat with one soft hand on top of the other, waiting for me to return with the change that he is only going to give back to me, but I let him repeat his little ritual of pushing the change dish towards me and saying, 'You keep that', after which I will thank him deeply for the tip, the *trink-geld*, which was traditionally money the waiter could use to have a drink at the end of his shift. But I don't drink much, and my shifts go on and on. The Pig shakes down one trouser leg and leaves the room.

'Not every day someone walks out on The Pig,' says the Bar Manager.

'You can say that again,' I say.

As though on cue, the Maître D' appears. He's always quickly on the scene whenever there's the slightest whiff of trouble.

'What's going on?' he asks. He'll stick his nose in now. He has to be in control. He thinks he owns the place, possibly because his father used to be the Maître D' here, and his father before him. I tell him the truth, with a neutral expression, that I'm not sure. He stares at me for a long moment and, as he so often does, slowly brings his big face closer to mine. As a rule, a child's face is a pure, rounded surface, the bearer of symbolic features: the eyes and the mouth. The eyes and the mouth are prominent on a child's face, a source of fascinating beauty, an interface for communication; you can read uncertainty, joy and sorrow in them. But, with age, the face becomes more and more dominated by the face itself. The eyes and mouth are thrown into the background by *the face itself.* The Maître D's face is a striking example of this 'triumph of the visage'. His eyes, which I'm sure were sparkling and clear at one point in time, are not only sunken and colourless, they're also oddly small in relation to the total surface area of his face. The bags beneath them make as much of a statement as the eyes themselves. Where his eyes and mouth were once responsible for the majority of his expressions when he was younger, they now make a minimal contribution to whatever else is 'going on' on his face. His mouth, once bursting, potent and soft, is tight and thin-lipped, surrounded by vertical lines which make him look like he is constantly playing the flute. What is left of his lips now functions more like shutters over his yellowed teeth. He has plenty of forehead, jaw and cheek, with hollows, pores and furrows, rough and slippery areas, oily surfaces. His face contains a wealth of shades and nuances, small webs of broken blood vessels, wear and tear from years of shaving, slapping on aftershave, and alcohol consumption. Certain expressions and grimaces have taken hold. It's easy enough to see, from the exterior, what's going on within, regardless of how buttoned up he is.

'Happiness and unhappiness live side by side,' he says.

Now, I can't really talk when it comes to appearance. If I want to meet my own concerns head-on, so to speak, then it's just a case of looking in the mirror. It's as though my face is a cast of all the anxieties that have built up within me over the years. I often feel stress and I know only too well its effects: tissue and subcutaneous fat are swept away by worry. I can feel the corners of my mouth being dragged down. A downward pull on my face, that's what I've got. I feel the emotions tearing at it. How can they do it? It's understandable that a drink problem can wear out and ruin a face, logical that the blood vessels and pores are widened by the alcohol – you can see all that playing out in the Maître D's face drama. But that emotions can ruin a face, well, that seems unfair. If you're nervous, you end up with a so-called nervy face. Try to conceal your nervy face with a poker face, and it only gets worse. What kind of evolutionary dead end is that? Nothing helps a nervy face.

'Sometimes,' says the Bar Manager, 'the Maître D' goes around the corner there to apply moisturizer. Hence the sheen.' I have to smile. 'He hides it well, but I can hear him rubbing it in.' We chuckle about that, the Bar Manager and me.

Audible rubbing in. 'But that,' she continues, 'isn't

something we can let Sellers and his group get wind of. They could spin an entire architecture of mockery out of a detail like that.'

* * *

Not long after three o'clock, a young woman comes in through the heavy curtains. She walks straight over to me and asks for Mr Graham, a.k.a. The Pig. Her voice is at once soothing and sharp, and she manages to squeeze a series of confirmations out of me. Mr Graham has gone? Yes. Were there others with him? Yes. Was there a middle-aged man with him? There was.

The girl looks like her picture on the phone, and I feel a faint sense of déjà vu. She is as fat, or should I say thin, as a model in a lifestyle magazine. Her self-confidence and air of naturalness could easily be mistaken for intelligence, and maybe it is intelligence. She looks like debauchery dressed up as asceticism. This may sound hair-raising, so forgive me, but I get the feeling that a person like her is a product of misogyny – and I mean that in a positive sense.

Not to be quirky here, but if you're familiar with Mathias Stoltenberg's portrait of the fifteen-year-old Elise Tvede, she's something like that. A version with fewer tangible concerns in her life, and surrounded by a kind of deafening contemporaneity. She is wearing an excellent Dries Van Noten outfit, and carries it off without effort, which is afforded to very few. Her feet are strapped into flawless Aquazurra shoes, with colourful little pompoms at the end of the straps. But, as they say, I think that behind all the elegance, there lies an *undethronable tackiness*. I believe this girl could be described as a commodity, even if I'm not sure what that's supposed to mean. What kind of figure are we dealing with here? The Hills is not the place for young blood. Is she The Pig's new flagship or something?

The Pig is careful with everything bordering on the so-called tasteless, including in the opposite sex. You can observe a steady supply of well-groomed women around him, but they're always of the well-established variety. Not the kind who carries the harsh glow of aspiration, in other words, and not the kind who cranes her neck and is driven by insatiable ambition. A woman who spends time with The Pig is a woman who has already mastered the game, a woman who does not give the impression of 'needing' The Pig and whom The Pig cannot 'use' at all – a woman who is The Pig's equal.

But the specimen standing before me now is a little young, is she not? Could she be a relative?

'Was there anything else?' I ask.

The girl stares at the mosaic on the floor. In the middle of each tile circle there are three stylized peonies in the palest of pinks. She looks up and suddenly seems ten years older.

'No, I'll come back. You can tell him I was here.'

'Mr Graham won't be back before tomorrow. Are you a Graham?'

'What?'

'Nothing. I beg your pardon.'

The girl has a cold glow, and when she thanks me and walks out, she leaves behind a vacuum, an absence that feels palpable. The Hills dims a couple of notches when she disappears through the curtain. As my friend Edgar often says: that kind of lumbar represents the last bastion of utility value. The Maître D' comes over and takes my arm, which is relatively awkward since I consistently hold my cards close to my chest in a work context.

'You shouldn't jump so high that you trip on your own beard,' he says, gesturing with one hand that I have a job to do.

I glance over to the Bar Manager. She has a questioning look on her face. Doesn't she know who the girl is either? It's rare for the Bar Manager to be at a loss about the customers. Her mental list of Oslo's café- and restaurant-goers is exhaustive. The Bar Manager is like an encyclopaedia. She takes an interest in and researches the clientele at The Hills like it's an academic field, or maybe some kind of hobby. She has so-called 'exhaustive knowledge' of the diners. She behaves like a vinyl collector with regards to who comes and goes. Her expertise can be irritating, in the way vinyl collectors are irritating, or in the way men with a deep knowledge of, say, bicycles are irritating, or men in photography shops, men being obsessively nerdy. To be fair, it should also be said that the Bar Manager occasionally shares information that I enjoy. Though rarely useful, it can offer one a kind of illicit thrill. But now she's standing there like the embodiment of a shrug.

Every Morning

Regularity and service act as a bulwark against inner noise. I work as much as I can. My days might seem endless, but that's how I want them. Every morning begins with me putting on my waiter's jacket. I take the white jacket from its hanger in the cramped changing room behind the kitchen. In with one arm, then the other, shrug it on to my shoulders. Horn buttons done up. Always the same. Sheer routine. I've had the jacket for eight years, at the very least. We get them from a manufacturer in Belgium that also makes military shirts. The jackets are of the highest quality, made from the same type of thin, plain-weave cotton fabric as the military shirts, and they're just as hard-wearing. The jackets have a row of horn buttons on the front, plus two small pockets. I use the right one exclusively for the bottle opener, the left is usually empty. The jackets do show wear, but in the nice way robust clothing does; the quality of the Hills interior is found again in the jackets. Both The Hills and these jackets are from a time when things had to be durable, and settle through use. Find their form. Not cheap and disposable, like most things today. 'The adornment of a city is manpower, of a body beauty, of a soul wisdom, of an object durability, of a speech truth,' Gorgias writes in the 'Encomium of Helen'. The part about the body is the only one which still applies, it seems. The durability of objects has been thrown overboard, at least. Some items hold up: the equipment the Head Chef surrounds himself with is durable, all of it. He avoids replacing things. As far as I know, he owns zero electronic gadgets. The fact that you constantly have to buy new electronic gadgets means that they aren't reliable and are thus a source of endless aggravation.

We have the jackets washed and pressed three times a week, and the aesthetic tension arising between a durable but worn piece of clothing and the rinsing and pressing of it, plus any possible starching, is irresistible. They use the same jackets at De Pijp in Rotterdam, the Majestic in Porto and the Fuet in Badalona, as well as at the old Kronenhalle in Zurich. The waiter's jacket is a standard uniform, and that suits me fine.

It's not so easy, the whole clothes thing. What do I wear when I'm not at work? Normal clothes. Deeply ordinary clothes. As Edgar says: the fact you have to get dressed every day means that, every day, you have to say 'yes' to the aesthetic choices made by a random designer, high or low on the company ladder, on either a good or a bad day. I often agree with Edgar, even if his reflections can be a bit grandiose. When I wear normal clothes, either on the way to or from work, I find myself falling into such a pattern of thought. My attention moves from the random designer behind my underwear to the man (usually a man) who has designed my navy-blue socks, the person who came up with my string vest, the everyday shirt on top of it, my trousers. I picture the designers. There they are, on good or bad days, designing clothes which I might pull up my legs or over my head before I go out, through town, heading straight to The Hills and home again, and in a way I'm giving them publicity, these clothes and their creators. I parade their business concepts all around town. That's not something I'm comfortable with. I'm not saying I'm much to look at, and I dress as neutrally as possible, but around one conference table or another, in one office or the next, the word 'neutral' has been given as the designer's motivation for this particular piece of clothing, and here I am, showing off this wretched designer's idea of 'neutrality', and that kind of thinking can fluster me.

And as though that wasn't enough, my thoughts then move on to shoes, watches, handrails and so on, into town, until that attitude also applies to façades, shop windows, road networks, food, movies and more. I walk around, stewing in my own juice, convinced that everyone is caught in a trap woven from everyone else's more or less successful aesthetic choices and clever ideas. Business ideas, pure and simple, conceived during more or less successful working days, and always driven by money. And it's this money-driven lobster trap that I'm caught in.

I wrap myself in a herring net of unnecessary business ideas every single day. I'm innocent in all of this. Not once have I asked for such a transaction, and not once have I forced such a transaction on to anyone else. Now I sound just like Edgar.

As a result, when I get to The Hills at a quarter to seven every morning, I can free myself from my 'self-chosen', 'neutral' clothes. I peel them off and pull on my uniform. It gives me breathing space. My relationship with the waiter's jacket is clear, because it has a time-tested design, with deep roots in tradition, meaning that it doesn't have to express some odd, cash-whipped jacket designer's generic idea of 'now', 'normality' or anything like that. I like the waiter's jacket, and I left it on a hanger in the back room yesterday, as neatly as possible, so that it would be ready to wear today. Ready to be pulled on, every morning, like clockwork. We go through the kitchen and into the wardrobe corner of the cramped changing room one by one and pull on our jackets. All the waiters and chefs take it in turn, aside from the Maître D'. He arrives ready dressed. I think he thinks the wardrobe corner is a bit nasty, a bit cramped. Which it is.

The kitchen at The Hills resembles a forge more than a kitchen. It's burnt, carbonized. The gas flame the Head Chef has burning in the corner looks like a furnace. The torching and sizzling has climbed up the walls and into every nook and cranny. His assistants stand at the other end of the kitchen; I don't have much to do with them. There is an opening between the kitchen and the restaurant, a combination of a hatch and some kind of kitchen island. It isn't something that was designed, rather it has grown organically over the past half-century, through use and additions. It's difficult to tell what's wall, what's shelf, what's pan hook and what's workbench or serving counter. The ceiling is as black as coke. The Chef sweats away beneath a ceiling so black that you don't even see it, it's virtually gone. There are more pots and pans and other utensils hanging above him, and above those is the ceiling, but you can't see that. He has stood there, the Chef, flambéing and flambéing, and he has burnt away the ceiling, so to speak. There's an absence, above the Chef's spot, a deep, dark void. That's how sooty it is. The ceiling reflects nothing. The kitchen is relatively cramped, and the Chef stands in the spot where the Head Chef stood before him, and the one before him, and has always stood, frying up this and that all day long, and, not least, flambéing those endless flambés.

His knives are lying clean and ready on a cloth to the right of the well-worn chopping board. There aren't too many of them, and each one has a limited area of use. They are, from an aesthetic point of view, a constant in relation to the Chef's robust build, while the purity of their steel is in sharp contrast to his harried face – something which links him, visually, even more closely to the knives. He's heavy-handed and lacks the gift of the gab. He's as big as a blacksmith himself, a boor with a God-given (but flat-bridged) nose for

30

gastronomy, a gorilla super-taster. He doesn't say much. When he first speaks, he's stiff and harsh. Like the time he mumbled that inside the Maître D', a civil war between alcoholism and homosexuality is being fought out.

I spread starched tablecloths on to the underlays and smooth them out with my hands. I wipe the marble surfaces. I wipe them even if they've already been wiped. I bring out water. I write the day's specials in chalk on the old board by the side of the kitchen hatch. I feel like a teacher when I do that. The papers have to be brought in. It's my job to sort them out every morning, and to put the long wooden clip on to the spines of each one, the so-called *Zeitungsspanners*. I hang them on the newspaper rail by the entrance. We don't offer the Norwegian daily papers in a place like this; they're too primitive. We try to maintain a continental standard. Instead, we hang up the few international papers still available in print editions. Not that we're desperately continental, but unfortunately offering the Norwegian papers simply isn't an option. They don't abide by the duty to provide information. From time to time, when it's quiet in here, I read one of the papers by the bar. There's no rushing through it on my part. I read carefully and turn the crisp pages slowly. Slowly making your way through the crisp pages of a broadsheet is an activity which, from a purely aesthetic point of view, is related to tailoring or playing the saxophone. In other words, related to a bygone era. Totally passé. Reserved for those with special interests. But it works perfectly. Call me old-fashioned, but changing what cannot be improved is also known as decline.

It's clean when I arrive at work. 'Clean'. The floors and surfaces are washed every night, but The Hills is in every respect a grubby restaurant. Engrained dirt. Not unhygienic, exactly, but it has to be said that it is a bit grimy in here, a little overgrown. All the years of food and fumes and breathing have essentially taken hold of the walls and formed a kind of film over the furniture and the little mosaic tiles, not to mention the ceiling. People used to smoke indoors, as one might remember, and the interior of The Hills still bears the marks of hundreds of thousands of cigarettes, from decade upon decade of smoking. The glasses and carafes are of the highest quality, traditional, not over-designed or flashy. The cutlery, as I might have already mentioned, is early Gebrüder Hepp, or original Puiforcat. The china has the characteristic Hills emblem in a Delft-blue glaze, with the perfectly drawn *H* wrapped in an oval at the top. I feel pepped up every time I place these plates on a table. That's what happens with good quality. It peps you up.

PART II

Edgar and Anna

I 'm not hugely fond of mixing roles, but I have grown accustomed to the following: a good friend of mine – well, one of my best friends – Edgar, whom I've mentioned before, comes here almost every other day. My best friend, actually. He always appears in the late afternoon, around five o'clock, and always with his daughter, Anna. I serve them like I do everyone else, but the atmosphere between us is different. To them, I'm both their waiter and friend. We always chat, or, rather, they talk to me while I work. Both are fairly talkative. Edgar is good at having opinions.

Edgar and I have known one another since we were seven or eight. He's the person I've known the longest. I always give Edgar and Anna the four-person table beneath the Per Krogh dog, so that Anna, who is nine, has space to do her homework to the side of the plates. A café table is, in many respects, the opposite of a school desk. Right? It's been said that the café table has been the most important place for so-called *bohemianist research* throughout European cultural history, the best place for a self-determined, autonomous study into how and when 'real life' is lived, or rather, how life 'is really lived'. *Research friendships* have been struck up or ended at the café table.

Anna pulls out books and a pencil case, sharpens her pencil until the shavings are everywhere, and gets to work. Despite Edgar's caustic opinions on having children – 'Because what Norway really needs is another highly sensitive kid, constantly clutching her iPhone' – he is fond of the girl. He has sole custody of her. The mother lives elsewhere, in another city. She's bipolar, got herself a serious benzodiazepine addiction and had her parental rights withdrawn following a period of eccentric and risky behaviour while Anna was a baby. I remember that Edgar was concerned about the mother's benzo intake during the first trimester of her pregnancy. Some reports suggest that the use of diazepam increases the risk of a cleft lip and palate. Anna has barely seen her mother. She does not, however, have a cleft palate, quite the opposite.

Anna stares at the bankrupt actor and whispers something to Edgar. The actor has a grotesque, unruly frizz of hair, which transitions into an equally frizzy beard. He looks like a Leonberger who's been drinking spirits for a hundred years.

Edgar says that they've been watching a programme in which various celebrities have to try to teach a class of twelve-year-olds. Some of them manage it well, others make a mess of it. Anna listens intently as Edgar tells me this, and grins when he gets to the parts she finds funny. Adult teeth appear at different rates at her age, but her teeth are brilliant white, regardless of their angle or length. Some children have slightly yellowed enamel on their new teeth, and that's not always quite so charming. Yellowed teeth in an uneven row, in a mouth full of obnoxiousness – I can do without that. Anna is polite and well turned out. Edgar is good at looking after her. Anna laughs loudly, and her laughter is so genuine that it's hard not to let yourself be charmed. She's as sharp as a knife.

There are a few golden years between infancy and the teenage years, Edgar says, when kids are as smart as they're ever going to be, or that's how it seems, but when they're still uncorrupted. Enormous resources are put into corrupting children at that age, according to Edgar. One institution, business model or technology after another is established solely to tame them and limit their potential. School grinds them down, Edgar always says. Organized activities bend and twist them in certain directions. Parents force them into one mould after another. Technology invades their worlds from an early age, presents itself as the law of nature and pulls at them with its temptations and illusions, trickling into their nervous systems, into their DNA, so that it, the technology, really does become the law of nature, and children can rarely or never again stand or sit with their full, uncorrupted potential, laughing loudly, with big belly laughs, the way Anna does now as Edgar talks about the TV programme.

Anna is *on her feet*, he's that funny. She points at him

and laughs because one of these celebrities-cum-teachers, Edgar says, has the misfortune of letting out the pupils' speckled dwarf hamster, which leads to complete chaos. The children squeal and run euphorically around the classroom, climbing the walls and falling over. In extreme slow motion come crystal-clear images of chairs tipping and pencil sharpeners opening mid-air, with their contents – the shavings – going everywhere. A desk is pushed over, and you can actually see a handful of crumbs from an eraser – rubbings – *scatter* across the floor in minute detail. Anna is completely absorbed. The celebrity teacher shuffles around, stooped over, trying to get hold of the little animal, which is running in terror from corner to corner. The scene is intercut with ones of the other seven celebrities all struggling to keep their respective classes in line. Edgar knows who only two of these people are, one an old folk singer he remembers from his childhood, and the other the poor, broke actor eating three tables away. The programme must have been filmed before his fraud was uncovered; he looks fresher and more in shape on the TV screen than in real life, out here in reality, Edgar says. I've always thought that The Hills is a good place for Anna, away from the screens, the monitoring, the schooling and the taming. The Maître D' is watching like a hawk, though. He comes over and says that I need to sweep up the pencil shavings which have fallen beneath Anna, or 'the girl', as he calls her.

Coffee

When I'm in a philosophical mood (invariably induced by Edgar), I reflect that coffee and driving share, in many respects, the same level of significance and the same metaphysical union with a 'free Western life'. The morning, as we all know, belongs to coffee. Regardless of the ripple effects that coffee production and motoring have, it's hard to imagine a life without the two, ideally in combination, and preferably in the morning. The activities of slurping coffee and driving cars are, in their very essence, linked to the idea of getting pumped up and under way: the bittersweet early morning with a coffee, or in the car, or with a coffee in the car, or with the car parked up outside the coffee place to get a coffee to have in the car. Or the old European café coffee which isn't linked to the car as such, but should be viewed as a stage of transportation which is also a destination in itself – the same way the car is always at once a mode of transportation and an end in itself.

Doing away with one of these is like amputating a limb from the body of society; it's completely out of the question. It's hard to see how the machinery of society is meant to 'get going' every morning without the two. 'Decaffeinated coffee is like kissing your sister,' someone once said. Isn't it typical that the only coffee quote I know is about decaf? The Bar Manager has put her foot down when it comes to serving decaffeinated coffee. It's simply not possible, she says. She's not some coffee fanatic, nor a caffeine fascist; she doesn't entertain any warped barista ideology, but she is old-school, and the line must be drawn somewhere, she claims.

The morning is mainly about coffee here at The Hills. It is also about croissants with jam, and the morning papers, but the coffee itself is the crux of the morning's activities. The Bar Manager is of the opinion that the cultural significance of coffee, in terms of both history and Realpolitik, should shine through our serving rituals. I myself have to be very careful with my coffee intake, but it's difficult to break the habit of a cup in the morning if one doesn't wish to distance oneself from a large and important community. Decaffeinated coffee is a surrogate for the feeling of belonging, pure and simple. You can still nurture the image of yourself as a coffee-sipping individual if the coffee is decaffeinated, but coffee is very much about caffeine, let's just put that out there – it's not just aesthetics and scene. Just think of *Schweigt stille, plaudert nicht* – Johann

Sebastian Bach's Coffee Cantata, which Johansen regularly plays up there on the mezzanine. I've heard that Voltaire drank fifty cups of coffee a day. I get very shaky from coffee. Sometimes, it tips me over into sheer paranoia. My being as one says 'highly sensitive' isn't a good fit with caffeine, it's one of the stimulants we highly sensitives react most strongly to. Other things we react to are noise and complex social contexts, the mixing of roles, hunger, and being given too many jobs to do at once. We can also quickly become *drained* in interactions with others, rather than gaining energy from them. I can't drink coffee before I get to work in the morning. The sounds, the chatter of the guests, it all becomes too sharp. I quickly grow dizzy and get palpitations; I get the feeling of impending internal collapse.

This isn't the place to bring up my personal history, but I recall one particular morning a few years back, a morning like today, the same time of year, with the same sunlight as now, falling obliquely into the restaurant over the coffee cups and morning papers on the worn marble table tops. I'd felt uppish and had been foolish enough to drink three or four cups of coffee before midday. I swung behind the bar, loaded up the machine and made myself one espresso after another. The intake of more caffeine can mitigate the comedown after too much coffee, and I had kept up that mitigation all morning, with the help of repeated espresso consumption. It was approaching half past one and I went to top up the cup of a gentleman sitting beneath the long mirror on the east wall.

My job has two key criteria: I have to show *pride in my work*, and I have to be *self-effacing*. The pride in my work makes me adhere to rigid routines which are vital for my well-being, since being highly sensitive entails that I don't like surprises or change. The self-effacing aspect means that I can interact with and serve people without having to get involved. In times like these, when there is so much bad taste about, it seems that taking responsibility, feeling pride in one's work and being self-effacing are all personal traits to be nurtured. So, with the coffee pot in hand, proudly and self-effacingly, I went over to the man sitting beneath the mirror. He was wearing the tie from hell, the pattern on it so busy that I lost my momentum and simply stood in front of him for a few seconds, completely unable to mobilize any of my standard phrases. And, as he stiffly asked for a refill, no doubt rather puzzled by my silence, I proceeded to collapse.

I still think it was his tie that caused it. An improbable weave of three shades of blue: an almost greyish Cambridge blue as the base, interspersed with stripes of duck-egg blue and topped off with speckles of what might have been periwinkle. The sight of his tie struck my retinas and made, physically, this house of cards of a nervous system that I have been dealt, and which had been fundamentally destabilized by my coffee drinking, come crashing down. I fell inwards, a slide and a fall. Everything became bright, and my head grew light as a helium balloon, felt like it was at once rising and falling. I had to hold out my free arm to avoid tipping over, and in so doing my hand brushed against an old woman's cheek and knocked against her table, making the cups rattle and the tea spill, as she sat cackling with her friend, completely unaware that I, her waiter, would come staggering in from one side like a character from a silent film and practically slap her soft, wrinkled cheek. I regained my balance, but I didn't dare try to apologize since my mouth felt lopsided, my tongue thick and heavy. So I stood there, blinking, swaying, the coffee pot still in my hand.

'Refill?' I asked, amazed that an actual word and not howls came out. My upper arms tingled.

'No, thank you,' said the man.

'I'll get someone to clean this up,' I said to the old women before walking out into the kitchen with long, nervous-breakdown steps, as though to find my sea legs against the dizziness. The little Filipino man with the floppy ears who did the washing-up then ran out with a cloth as I uttered the words 'spill' and 'table 14'. What was his name again? I stood on the inside of the swing doors, breathing through my nose and squeezing my hands until they regained feeling. Bayani, I think it was, Baiany, Bajanwi. Anyway, the Chef was flambéing away repetitively beneath the carbonized ceiling. He poured cognac into the sauté pan and deftly caught a flame from the gas hob so that a fireball was thrown up from the copper pan. The blue alcohol flame against the golden copper looked amazing. He's an aesthete, the Chef.

These days, I try to limit my coffee consumption to a single cup in the afternoon.

Eyeballs

Well, what do you know? Here she comes, gliding across the mosaic tiles in casual flat shoes: it's the young woman whom The Pig and his companions were waiting for the other day. This early? Is it breakfast she wants? Now, I may be mistaken, but it feels like some kind of 'bidding round' takes place every time she comes in. Isn't it called a Giffen Good, a product that paradoxically grows in demand as its price rises? It's like the young woman has a similar quality. I don't know.

She sits down and glances over at me. She moves her head back almost imperceptibly. Just a slight raising of the chin. And what a chin. I react quickly and go over with two menus.

'Are you waiting for anyone else?'

'No.'

'Coffee?'

'Yes, please.'

For a moment, I think about asking whether she finally got hold of The Pig, but I bat that notion away, slightly shocked that I'm even considering it. It's far beyond my job description to press and question the guests. One can suddenly put one's foot in it. She could be a grandchild, she could be a business contact or an erotic liaison for all I know. The guests shouldn't have to explain themselves in here. But you do think about these things. She must be some kind of asset, otherwise she wouldn't be in circulation. A resource for The Pig. Credit. What does the Bar Manager know about her? Very little, it seems. She stands there, with her intelligent face, looking like a question mark.

It seems unfair that we always have to describe their appearance first when describing girls, but what can I do? It's all I have. The impression the young woman makes is absorbing. I hand her one of the menus, clutching the other to my ribs. I stand there for a bit too long. She's reading, and I'm staring straight at the top of her head. A not-quite-straight parting runs from her crown down to her left temple, where her fringe is pushed to the right and then falls over her face. She is leaning forward, studying the menu.

Edgar had an affair with a girl once. She drove him crazy. Even though she always showed him complete affection, Edgar said, and showered him with the sense that he was supreme in a way he had never experienced with any other partner – he had believed her and her shower of compliments completely – he was also eaten up by the suspicion that he wasn't the only one being given that treatment.

'Could I have a little milk in my coffee?' the girl says with some kind of smile.

Edgar never managed to prove anything. He never caught her flirting or cheating in any way, but the fact that her radiance had had such a magical effect on him from the very outset could only mean, Edgar argued, that it also had a similar effect on others. And the thought that she, that person who had made him feel so unique, perhaps for the very first time, might not in fact have been exclusively his, made him boil over. The fact that she struck *him* in that special way, and might potentially strike all the *others* in the same way, made him blow a fuse. The greediest, most egotistical and unkind sides of Edgar came out then, he had said, and grew uncontrollably, like weeds, like wheatgrass, with their long, creeping and far-reaching roots. He related to her the way a capitalist relates to his pot of money, he said. Like a hawker. Stingy. I never met her, but I've developed an image of her in my mind from the hours I spent listening to Edgar's woes at the time, and that image materializes in the young woman now sitting before me at The Hills. She's just how I imagined her. A generator of jealousy. The girl looks up at me, and I realize that she's wondering what's happened to her coffee, because now she hands me the menu and asks for the cereal with lime-blossom honey and goat's-milk yoghurt.

'And the coffee, too.'

I hurry out to the kitchen, my back straight. It might sound funny, but that's exactly what I do: I hurry across the floor. I hurry through the swing doors and out into the kitchen, grab one of the coffee pots and immediately return with it in one hand and a petite steel milk jug in the other. The jug is so small that I have to hold the handle between my thumb and index finger. I rush over to the young lady and pour the coffee. Then I subtly lift the milk jug while I look at her and raise my eyebrow almost imperceptibly, as though to suggest the question: 'Would you like a drop of milk in your coffee?'

'Yes, please,' she replies to my gesture, and I pour an amount of milk which couldn't be described as anything but a dash. I give her another questioning look and she says, 'A little more', and, with my little finger pointing upwards and out because of the tiny jug, I pour another dash.

'One moment, and I'll fetch you one of today's papers,' I say, but she stops me and says that's not necessary. No papers? All right. What kind of person do we have here?

'Wonderful,' I say.

Really? Not interested in the papers in the morning? I see. I can sometimes be blinded by the notion of an old Europe that's being nurtured and preserved here at The Hills, but I'm still taken aback that she can't yield to the tradition of rustling a broadsheet over a coffee in the morning light. What does she mean, it's not necessary? Physical newspapers are increasingly being swapped for other equipment in here, even in the morning, I've noted that. I'm not saying there's any kind of betrayal in fishing out a device rather than rustling the paper, all I'm saying is that it's noted. But the young lady doesn't pull out any form of technology. She just sits there, as though on show, sipping her coffee with calm movements.

As I walk around scraping up crumbs, I follow the girl out of the corner of one eye, taking in everything she does or, more accurately, everything she doesn't do. She continues her sipping, but otherwise there's very little to write home about. My favourite activity is using the crumber to scrape the crumbs from the tables. We have both crumbers and so-called crumb brushes at the restaurant, and I prefer the crumber. I deftly push the crumbs on to the crumb tray I'm holding beneath the edge of the table. I hang the crumber back in its place and go over to the young woman. With the venerable *New York Times* in my hands, not some paper from the nervous, old Europe, I'll have you know, but one of the papers that, ironically enough, maintains a sense of the old Europe. It has about it an aura of the twentieth century. I hand her a fresh, crisp copy.

'That's not necessary,' she says again.

'Thank you,' I say.

Why am I pushing newspapers on to the guests? Thank you? I put down the eternal *New York Times*, grab the crumber again and run it over the tablecloths with experienced hands. I even run it over the tops of the tables I've already scraped, doubling the amount of work for myself.

'Excuse me,' the girl says, signalling that she wants to pay. I immediately present her with the bill. While she fishes out the cash from a becomingly cluttered handbag, I suggest that it looks like a lovely day.

'Hmm,' says the girl.

When she gets up, it sinks in how hideously well proportioned she is. Symmetrical. I saw it yesterday, but I hadn't taken it in. Now I take it in. There's a male guest who is firmly in his mid forties two tables away, and he can't control his eyeballs as she straightens up and stretches, before swinging a light autumn coat – is it angora? – over her shoulders, a light jacket, a crocheted jacket? A knitted jacket? Was it knitted on thick needles? Is it homemade, was it made on a machine? An organic, long-waisted, hand-knitted jumper camouflaged as a jacket? A cosy angora? The eyeballs of the man two tables away have taken on a life of their own. It's interesting to watch a man whose eyeballs are out of control.

That said, I should look at my own eyeballs before I start talking about other people's. Mine are running amok as much as his. The difference is that my eyes are seeking out his for brief moments, as though they want to confirm that he (his eyeballs) is seeing what I (my eyeballs) am seeing. The man's eyeballs are engaged in a battle with his will, which is trying to keep them to himself, but the eyeballs are drawn to the girl like two owlets as she stands there stretching and pulling on her jacket. Then she walks towards the door, a journey which sucks the air from the room, re-establishing some of that vacuum she leaves in her wake. With elegant, possibly self-objectifying steps, she disappears through the curtains. She reappears on the outside of the arched windows, which are covered at the bottom with lace curtains on brass poles. She disappears behind the wall again, reappears in the next window, disappears behind the wall, and continues like that along the entire row of windows, off and on, like a film strip.

'Like all slaves, girls think they're watched more than they really are,' the man with the eyeballs mutters, glancing at me. What does he mean by that? He should pull in his eyeballs before they roll out of their sockets. I see that the swindler actor has already taken his seat. And, on cue, old Johansen starts playing the piano up on the mezzanine – he gives us Bach, and Goldberg Variation No. 5, up-tempo. These small occurrences mean that the time is almost exactly ten in the morning.

'I'll have a vodka,' says the actor.

'Would you prefer Belvedere,' I ask, 'or Reyka?' That's the Icelandic vodka I know he drinks from time to time.

The actor breathes out like a whale; it seems as though life itself is leaving his body. He then inhales in such a way that his nose whistles, before he lets the air go again and growls, 'Belvedere' with a voice so sonorous you might think it had seeped out of the bowels of hell.

I exchange a few words with the Bar Manager – if I have to chat, she's the person I choose. She tells me she had some unfortunate trouble with the timing belt, as it's known, in her car yesterday afternoon. On a separate note, I learn that the Rwandan Twa people are, interestingly enough, potters, something which is unusual among pygmy peoples. And would you believe it, the Bar Manager has managed to get her hands on a lovely little Twa pot.

'Listen, the young lady, who is she?' I ask out of the blue.

'The rapist,' the Bar Manager says cryptically, the way she often does when she owes me an answer, 'is not fighting with either man or woman, but with sexuality itself.'

'What?'

The Pig Wants to Talk

The Pig arrives at half past one on the dot and sits with his hands in his lap. He is too decent, too tasteful, too refined to fiddle with his phone at the table. There's something unrefined about checking text messages and social media. If you have to pull out your phone and 'check' it constantly, you're a child or some kind of tart – yes, let that sound as petty as you like. Independent, balanced people with a certain status don't do it. But then I have the misfortune of telling The Pig that the young woman he was waiting for yesterday was here, not just yesterday but earlier today too, thereby forcing the venerable Pig on to his phone.

'She was here earlier today?' His eyes widen.

'Yes.'

'Did she ask after me?'

'Not today.'

'And yesterday?'

'Yes, she asked yesterday.'

'Would you excuse me a moment?'

From the inside pocket of his suit jacket (impeccable), not the pocket of his trousers (spotless), he pulls out his phone (depraved). He proceeds to jab at it. Will he call, I wonder, or will he send a message? So far, so interesting. I pay attention. Will he use his fingers or his voice to communicate what needs to be communicated? He taps the screen with his fingertips. From where I'm standing, it's impossible to tell whether he is bringing up a number or whether he's typing. He half turns to me, gestures 'two minutes' and heads to the exit. As he disappears behind the curtain, the draught excluder, the fabric covering the door, he lifts the phone to his ear. Interesting. I watch him outside as he lights a cigarette. He walks up and down the street for three minutes as he breathes in tobacco smoke, drag after drag, and talks on the out-breaths. His right hand, which is holding the filterless cigarette, gestures calmly between inhalations. When he comes back in, he says: 'Right.'

I fetch the bottle of white burgundy, which I swiftly open with the corkscrew I keep in the right-hand pocket of my jacket. I pour.

'There will be three of us today, not four,' says The Pig. And then, 'You know, there was something I'd like to discuss with you.'

I clear the unneeded fourth setting from the table.

'What is it?'

'I've wanted to mention it to you for a while.'

53

'I beg your pardon?' I say as my face warms up.

'You know,' says The Pig. 'You know when Peter Norton bought the letters Joyce Maynard put up for auction at Sotheby's in 1999 . . .'

'Peter Norton,' I say.

'Yes, fourteen letters and notes from 1972 and 1973, in which Salinger, among other things – ironically – warns young Joyce Maynard against fame and exploitation . . .'

'I'm sorry,' I say.

'Norton's intention in buying the letters – they went for well over 150,000 dollars, double the estimate – was to give them back to Salinger, so that he could do what he liked with them, lock them away in a safe, burn them . . .'

'I'm sorry,' I say. 'I have to see to the other tables.'

'But there's something I really want to discuss with you . . .'

'Excuse me,' I say.

'Norton was also after one of Holbein's more obscure Tudor drawings which was on sale at the same auction . . .'

'You'll have to excuse me.'

'When does your shift finish?' asks The Pig.

'At five, but then I have to go straight to a meeting.'

'I see.'

I never have meetings. I'm always at work. What was that all about? I have to do my job now. Where's the crumber? Tables 5 and 12 have gone, I need to de-crumb them. I quickly clear the tables, find the crumber and run it over the tablecloths with energetic movements. Now 7 and 3 have left. I take payment for 19. Table 11 wants more mineral water, and 4 sends back a Loosen Bros. Riesling. What was all this talk about Salinger and Maynard? Holbein? The Bar Manager hints that table 3 will be getting new guests. The two people keeping The Pig company at his usual table 10 also arrive. I escort them over; one is a colleague of The Pig's, a sharp-nosed, vulture-like figure called Årvoll; the other is his polite, but slightly startled-looking daughter. I recognize both of them from previous occasions. I fill their glasses. For nineteen years, we've kept things professional, The Pig and I. Why this sudden eagerness? I keep in continual motion until the clock strikes five, at which point I quickly get changed. I have to get out, away from the eager Pig, who is still sitting here three and a half hours later – likely full of questions about Maynard and Salinger – sipping his never-ending burgundy. He studies the greasy smears of alcohol sliding down the glass. I have to get away from him.

Ill-treatment of Animals

'Should I ask the Chef to fry you some onion?' I ask two days later.

'No, thank you,' says Anna.

Edgar looks at Anna and points to the beef patties with a surprised expression. 'But if you're having the beef pa—'

'No onion,' insists Anna.

The Chef rinses the chopping board and peels, cuts and fries the onion. That this vegetable has been used for thousands of years is strange, and that the ancient Egyptians *worshipped* it is hard to believe, in my opinion. Is it because concentric skins and multiple layers symbolize 'eternal life' or 'the solar system'? I remember some of my friends from childhood used to call immigrants 'onion Jews'. That was funny. Onions weren't used in cooking in the countryside where I grew up. The Chef shovels the fried onion on to a medium-sized plate, and I place it in front of Edgar so that the restaurant logo is precisely at twelve o'clock.

'Thanks,' he says. 'You don't want any?'

I shake my head. He knows I never eat at work. 'I'm not too keen on onions.'

'Me neither,' says Anna.

'In the past, people thought onions made them strong,' I say.

'How strong?'

'Strong strong. Gladiators rubbed onion on to their muscles to make them stronger. In the Middle Ages, people paid their rent with onions.'

'Now you're being silly,' says Edgar.

'I'm not.'

'Could you pay with onions in a shop?' Anna wonders.

'I don't know. Maybe they didn't have shops. But you could get your hair to grow back if you went bald. They made you strong. And potent.'

'What's "potent"?' asks Anna.

'Getting an erect penis,' says Edgar.

'Why would you want that?'

'And think of the poor Indians. We took the onion to America,' I say.

'We?'

'Europeans. We found potatoes, turkeys, gold and tobacco over there. And coffee. And cocaine. And bananas. We brought it all back home. And we took the onion over with us. What did the Indians make of that?'

'They probably don't like onions.'

'But now there aren't any Indians,' says Edgar.

'Yes, there are,' says Anna. 'Catarina in my class is an Indian.'

'Where is she from?'

'Venezuela.'

'She's probably mixed-race,' says Edgar.

'I don't know, but she's got a lisp,' says Anna.

'She lithpth?'

'Yeth, she lithpth.'

'The Thpanish do that too. It meanth that she hath Thpanish blood in her veinth.'

'I thee,' Anna says seriously.

'Venethuela,' says Edgar.

Edgar rubs the bridge of his nose, and makes a slight smacking sound with his right eye. After that, he clears his throat and blinks until his eye refocuses. Edgar is tired of me. I ask whether Anna still eats meat. Edgar points to the beef patties. I point out that once, she talked about how meat was disgusting because of the ill-treatment of animals. Edgar has money in the bank, I know that. He doesn't have an appendix, I know that, too. Edgar can come out with things like: 'In everyday speech, "meat" is the muscle and fatty tissue from slaughtered animals which is sold as food for humans', and then pull a meaningful expression, as though he's revealed something. As though he has single-handedly uncovered the perverseness of fetishizing one's food intake. Edgar can be so conceited. He talks away. The ill-treatment of animals is one thing, he says. But what does that abuse say about the people looking after the animals?

It's time for an explanation. He wets his lips. Edgar takes it upon himself to talk about an article he read, on a new book written by an author whose starting point was a news report recounting the Society for the Protection of Animals' investigations into the welfare of animals on Norwegian farms. 'And imagine,' says Edgar, 'the Society says that serious abuse often testifies to the farmer's depression or mental breakdown. In other words, the neglect of animals is almost always a sign of human breakdown.' The book he is referring to is a novel, and the trick in the novel – 'Listen,' says Edgar – is to depict a farmer's mental collapse *from the animals' point of view.* An *Animal Farm* of psychiatry, if you like. The farmer was a bachelor, aged forty-seven. The pigs were thirsty. Things dragged on. What was he doing? The only one who had any contact with him was the cat, which moved freely in and out through the cat flap, and sat on his lap. The TV was on, as usual. The dog was complaining from its kennel. Its lead reached almost to the kitchen window, but it couldn't see in.

The sheep were freezing. It was early November. For seven whole days they had stood outside. The snow hadn't arrived yet, but there was frost in the mornings, and it was bitingly cold. A couple of them had diarrhoea and got muck on their wool. There were howls from the pigpen. The sow had licked and nibbled at one of the piglets so much that it was dark and looked like a seal cub. What about the hens? Two had been pecked to death, and one was featherless and covered in open sores. The other hens skipped past it and dealt out heartless bites and nips. The author had done her research thoroughly, Edgar argues, because there were details in the book that she couldn't possibly have made up. Edgar himself has worked on a farm, he says, and knows how long it takes before, for example, a horse becomes dehydrated or, say, the pigs turn on one another. The book was well written, in Edgar's opinion. Conceptually comprehensive and not at all over the top. And that wasn't an easy task, given that the book's point of view is the animals', and, as we know, animals have no language. How do you describe the feeling of starvation felt by a cow? Cows have five stomachs but no vocabulary. What should an author write when, through the emotional register of a mistreated pig, she needs to describe confusion and fear? Edgar hadn't thought anyone would manage it before he began reading, but the author had certainly found a clever solution to that particular narrative problem. No solutions to Edgar's endless lectures are mentioned.

Transport

I think with horror about all the shipping, all the transportation, the truly endless transportations, which must have happened for Blaise to be sitting here, glittering, at The Pig's usual table 10, raising an espresso cup to his lips. Where does the marble beneath the tablecloth come from? Bolzano? Where is the porcelain from? Hungary? His suit is from London, or rather the cutting and stitching were done in London. The fabric comes from here, the lining from there. The tie might be Scottish; it's a tartan. I recognize the cufflinks, they're from a big French fashion house. His shoes are from Lombardy, I've noticed, and his socks, believe it or not, I recognize as American. He bought the socks from Neiman Marcus. And so on. I know that Blaise gets his hair cut by João Fuentes, the Portuguese hairdresser and stylist, at a salon called Federer. The hairdresser has flown in from Portugal, while Blaise's socks came flying in from the USA. And so on.

Then there's the coffee. The beans are dragged, heaved, driven and shipped all the way from Bolivia. It's a claustrophobic thought, that the only thing in my field of vision right now, here at The Hills, as I stand looking at Blaise and his constituent parts – the only thing from Norway is the splash of milk in the little steel jug. But the cow was still milked up in the hills somewhere, by a farmer, mentally ill or not, and the milk, it was transferred to a tanker and sloshed and jostled down the milk route towards the capital just so it could end up in the petite Gebrüder Hepp milk jug that I've placed in front of him. Everything is dragged in.

The overall experience of a *Grand European* in central Oslo is of a patchwork without parallel. It's made possible by plundering items from every corner of the world; they've trawled the ends of the earth for the ingredients and the means, raw materials – and ideas. Because the idea itself is, of course, from Vienna, or Paris, or possibly Berlin, with some influence or other from the pubs and dives in Amsterdam or Rotterdam, to which the Norwegians have had access over the years as a result of their sea travel. But at the same time, The Hills is one of the capital's defining and most historic institutions, one that gives Oslo its character. The space, or the premises, where I now and will for ever stand in my waiter's jacket, is an intricate mesh of scraped-together items, and I sometimes feel sick at the thought that the most long-standing, constant, so-called traditional and unchanging place is a mosaic of items dragged and scraped together.

I often think about all the shipping routes that are

established, maintained and worn out, which lead to The Hills from all directions, so that the spoils can find their way here, to The Hills, and down into the cellar and up into the kitchen, to be carried by me to the tables, right over to Blaise's marble-top. They point from every corner of the world, to Europe, to northern Europe, to Oslo, to The Hills. Early morning here, with this level of tradition and quality, would not be possible without the tankers, suburban depots, railway sidings, loading ramps, cradles, lorries, bleach buckets and containers, pallets and cranes. How much land, how many stretches of Europe and the rest of the world are torn apart, slumified and buried under traffic, with all the wear and tear that transport brings, so that Blaise can repeatedly lift his espresso cup to his lips and feel a sense of belonging to something European, is anybody's guess. It's through transport that civilization is established, of course, and it's through transport that civilization will go under, I should think, or at least that's what Edgar thinks. Anyway. I digress.

Out of the vans and down into the cellar go the goods. Everything goes down to the cellar. Via the trapdoor or the loading window. The men who do the deliveries push two loading rails into the hatch and let the boxes slide down. What is the name of that piece of equipment? I once asked one of them while they were lifting cartons.

'What do you call those rails?'

'No idea,' he said.

So, the equipment has no name. Down into the cellar it goes, in any case.

Mix-up

Frigidity, someone once said, is the truth behind nymphomania. Impotence is the truth behind Don Juanism. And anorexia, well, that's the truth behind bulimia. I can't remember who said it, but I think about those words as the irrepressible young lady who asked after The Pig makes yet another entrance. The curtain moves to one side. Here she is. 'Herself', 100 per cent, but also painfully generic. After only a few days, she has become the most frequent guest at the establishment. What does she want? With a choppy, *Zeitgeist*y stride, she heads in the direction of the Maître D', who is bent over the reservations book, fuming. She smiles with her full dental arch.

She's too early this time, it's only quarter past one, fifteen minutes before The Pig's table needs to be ready. And yet again, she brings with her a feeling of déjà vu, stronger today. Her power. Her posture, the squeezing together of her shoulder blades. Her shoes. The intelligent contradictions of her outfit. She makes the room light up. My workplace immediately becomes a stage, an arena. At the same time, it's as though she drags all of The Hills' grandeur, age and long-standing diligence down to the level of her hip bone. The Hills is an eatery, but in many ways this girl expresses a hatred of flesh, a fantasy of the fundamentals of anatomy – the skeleton. She's on the phone.

'Oh God, you're *gross*!' She continues to smile.

With three fingers over the handset, she asks the Maître D' about Mr Graham. The Maître D' tells her – with help from a mouth which is more a taut ring, a sphincter, than two separate lips, and a couple of bent fingers suggesting the direction – that The Pig's table will be ready in five minutes. Would she kindly take a seat at the bar until then?

The talkative Bar Manager, owner of a brand-new timing belt and an elegant Twa pot, is standing with her spine as straight as a spear and asks her firmly what she would like. The girl gives her a blank look, as though there were water in front of her eyeballs, and places her order. And this is when the plot thickens. I pay close attention to this: she asks for a quadruple espresso. The Bar Manager doesn't exactly widen her eyes – she's a professional – but you can see that she has an opinion on the matter. She goes straight over to the machine and pours one espresso on top of another, until it's a quadruple. I've paused with the crumber and watch the Bar Manager fill an ordinary coffee cup to the brim with espresso: it's a shocking sight.

The very thought of the espresso being a quadruple makes me sweat. I stare at the girl's face. She sips. How to describe that sipping? In a time like ours, as Edgar says, when the existing political language is unable to offer any solution other than keeping people's suffering at a distance through control, increased consumption, white health, extreme tourism and entertainment, how should I describe this girl's drinking of a quadruple espresso? There is no political language to express the conflicts of our age. But this much I can say: the girl drinks the coffee as though it's *me* who should be drinking it. Does that make sense? She drinks it with a kind of outward pleasure. I *feel* the espresso as *she* drinks it. The cup, made from quality stoneware, placed on an adorable saucer, is raised to her mouth with hypnotizing calm. The small clouds of steam – or whatever it is that rises from hot coffee – produce some kind of receptive, inviting 'breath' which, how should I put it, 'sells' the coffee to me. The quadruple espresso is sold to me, the highly sensitive, by the espresso itself, aided by the girl's interaction with it. What kind of agent is she? What is her product? It seems like the Bar Manager needs a shot herself – she's watching just as intently as I am.

He's well off, The Pig, with plenty to keep him busy. The business of being prosperous, that's what he does, on a day-to-day basis. Everyone he surrounds himself with plays one role or another in this activity. It's crucial that the demonstration of this practice and maintenance of wealth is done with class. The conversation taking place between three ordinary money-men on table 7, for example, would never be heard from The Pig's table:

'*He's a fool . . . he benched the boat at 13. You know how much salt's on the litre? He came down with pure slush, PURE slush.*'

With perfect timing and a whip-like motion, the young girl downs the last of her coffee as The Pig comes through the curtain, with Blaise Engelbert hot on his heels. It looks like Blaise is uncomfortable with that order, as though he's never walked behind another person before. But The Pig, without being some kind of shameless alpha male, has a natural authority (or is it slyness?) which means he consistently thrusts his right shoulder in front of Blaise as they approach the Maître D', as they are shown to the table.

I act like an idiot by saying '*voilà*' to the young woman to indicate that her companions have arrived, but she's already worked that out. I, the Bar Manager and the Maître D' stand idly by, watching her slide off the bar stool, grab her bag and her seamless (not literally, it does have seams) jacket. With confident, firm steps, she walks over to The Pig and his associate. The Pig and Blaise spot her at the same moment, and they let go of the backs of their chairs and napkins and turn to her 'like flowers towards the sun', as my grandmother would have put it. They are ready and waiting, and the girl hugs them in descending age order – The Pig first, then Blaise. She isn't related to either of them, that much is clear. The fawning and fuss The Pig and Blaise make over her aren't something you do with your nearest and dearest. And a grandchild would never be so coquettish with their grandfather. She seems rushed, breathless, as though the clock is ticking. Why such a hurry? Maybe she's buzzing from the quadruple espresso. She is like a flapping fish, fresh food demanding to be consumed because she is approaching her expiry date with every passing moment.

The Pig's table is mine. Maybe it would have been appropriate to pull out a chair for the young lady, but I hang the crumber on its hook and start to shuffle the menus instead. 'Madam,' I say. It's hard to tell whether she's a lady or a girl. Child or lady. She's some kind of child lady. In every respect, she's an 'adult'. Definitely 'adult' in appearance, as well as in her habits, which are far too refined to belong to a child, not to mention expensive. But the youthful tenderness, the slightly underdeveloped impression of being fresh, seems cultivated, and in a knowing rather than innocent way. A professional way. Dare I say a speculative way?

'The thinnest string makes the finest music,' the Maître D' says, giving me an unreadable look from behind his eye bags. I know I have to take their drinks order. The Maître D' shouldn't have to make an effort with glances and so on. I hasten over.

'What do you know,' The Pig says with a smile, indicating that a bottle of white burgundy would be appropriate.

I hand out the menus clockwise, starting with Child Lady. Not to boast, but the way I elegantly open the cover with one hand, straight to the lunch page, and hand it to her at a comfortable reading angle, is both quick and smooth: experienced. She looks up at me and nods. Blaise gets his menu last, and I don't open his since he's sitting at an awkward angle to the right; Blaise gets a closed menu.

'Would you like me to go through the specials?' I say.

'No, thank you,' says The Pig.

'Let me just say that the plaice is very good today.'

'Thank you.'

Let me just say? What is it with my brazenness? Didn't The Pig say no? The plaice is completely ordinary today. What am I talking about? I go over to the bar and ask the Bar Manager for two brandies. She quickly pours two Stravecchios and I place one in front of The Pig and one in front of Blaise. The Pig politely turns to me as he takes off his menu glasses.

'What is this?' he says.

'Stravecchio,' I say.

'What?'

I feel a muscle twitching in my neck and apologize.

'I'm so sorry, it must be a mistake. A mix-up.' I shake my head, pick up the glasses of brandy and return them to the bar.

'Was it off?' the Bar Manager asks. She opens the Stravecchio and sniffs it. Grinding my jaws, I sway on the spot and continue shaking my head.

* * *

'Who is she?' I whisper, right into the Bar Manager's ear, like a sleazebag.

'What can I say . . .' she says with a knowing look on her face. 'We can try to work it out.'

'Let's.'

She holds up three slim, unmanicured fingers, and racks her brain.

'I think Graham is three-score years. How old do you think the girl could be? One? One-and-a-half-score? She can't be any more than one-and-three-quarters. There's no way. And no younger than one-score. Could she? Seven-eighths? No. She must be a full score, at the very least. I'll be damned if she's a teenager. I'd guess she's one-and-a-half, but it's hard to tell. As you can see for yourself, any assumptions about her age bounce off her face like water off a duck's back.'

'That's for sure,' I say.

'Graham's daughter is well over thirty and is studying in London, we know that. It's not her.'

'No.'

'And she doesn't have a twenty-year-old child.'

'No.'

'As far as we know, Blaise doesn't have any children, and definitely not any grandchildren. He's barely over fifty.'

'She could be a stepchild of Blaise's? Katharina's daughter from a previous relationship?'

'No, Katharina has a son. And look how they're behaving. They're not family.'

'I noticed that,' I say.

The Bar Manager alternates between twirling the espresso tamper in her fingers and weighing it in her hand, level with her belt buckle. Her gaze is fixed somewhere beyond the horizon. I'm waiting for some kind of continuation.

'Like someone said,' she says, 'war is the most intelligent form of irrationality.'

'Did they?'

'Yeah, a hundred years ago . . .'

'That's something to ponder,' I say.

'That comes to me when I look at the girl.'

'Ah.'

'There's something agitating about her, not exactly bellicose, but provoking, inflammatory.'

'Don't you have anything more concrete?'

'I have found an odd detail,' says the Bar Manager.

'Go on.'

'It's not often that pretty women have nicknames. Elegant women have names like Jasmine, Caroline, Cameron, Mia, Billy, Cindy, Flannery, Mira. But this one has a nickname.'

'Oh?'

'They call her Zloty. She has a proper name, but people call her Zloty.'

'You're kidding.'

'No, that's what I've heard.'

'But who is she?'

'One thing at a time. Behave yourself, now.'

* * *

71

The Bar Manager winks at me as she says, 'Behave yourself, now.' It's a bit much. She needs to calm down. She can't throw that kind of accusation around. I grab a rag I have no use for. I glance at the crumber. Should I go to the kitchen? Should I top up the Stravecchio? A slight dizziness strikes me; a few seconds fold in on themselves and disappear, and I experience a moment of confusion. My field of vision grows cloudy.

Then I'm back, and my years-long routine of waiting on The Pig kicks in. The Pig doesn't need to signal when he's ready to order; I know when The Pig is ready. I can feel it. I head over to his table. With his back to me, he starts to dictate into thin air – he knows I'm there.

'We'll take two bottles of the usual, not one. More mineral water, and' – The Pig turns to Child Lady – 'perhaps you would like to start?'

She stares at the menu, shakes her head and passes her turn, the wrong way, to her right, where Blaise is sitting.

'It's a bit early for kid, isn't it?' Blaise says, smiling broadly as he glances around. 'I'll take the snails. Give me a couple extra, and that'll do.'

'Of course,' I say.

'I'm always surprised by how filling snails are.'

I think Blaise has just had his hair done. Goodness me, is that threading I can see at the edge of his beard? No, such a tasteful man would never do that. That's the kind of thing they do in the Middle East. I will assume his beard line is naturally strong and well defined.

72

Now he changes his mind, as he often does.

'Are there really herbs from the Nordmarka forest on the plaice?' he asks, looking at me as though longing for a concise answer.

'Absolutely,' I say, meeting his steady gaze so as to leave no doubt about the herbs.

'Then I'll try the plaice instead.'

'The plaice is an excellent choice.'

'I can never get the hang of snail tongs, anyway.'

The Pig nods appreciatively, though it isn't appreciation for Blaise in his nod, more a kind of confirmation that the choreography of the ordering is going well, despite Blaise's dithering. Now he directs our attention back to Child Lady, who is still staring at the menu. I hold a small, spade-shaped hand in the air by her face. She could have turned around and gagged on it. With a gentle *plop* she closes the menu and stares straight ahead, the way she did before the quadruple espresso, with water hazing her eyes.

'Could you fry me up a selection of mushrooms? But no oyster mushrooms,' she says, her voice sounding a little croaky.

There's a slight rise in the floor, in the mosaic, by the entrance to the rotunda (it isn't actually a rotunda, but we call it one anyway), and I've unintentionally placed my right foot on that rise which means that I have a slight, awkward, forward lean as I give her a nod which conveys certainty, despite the nodding ban.

'The kitchen will take care of it.'

73

I pull back my leg and move my still-spade-shaped hand towards The Pig's face.

'I'll take the tartare, but with only a dash of grapeseed oil, as you know.'

'Wonderful,' I say, gathering the menus in a clockwise direction.

The Chef gets to work like an automaton, immediately chopping and frying mushrooms, finishing them off with a quick flambé. Once he has arranged the mushrooms, the plaice and the tartare on plates bearing the restaurant emblem, I take the first two on my right arm, balance the last one on my left, and go out and place the mushrooms in front of Child Lady, the tartare in front of The Pig, and then, inexplicably, the plaice in front of the inebriated actor at table 9. Blaise stares at me in bewilderment. The Pig makes a strange movement with his hand, but doesn't say anything. No one touches their food. The table is completely silent. I draw it out, let the silence become piercing, before I retrieve the fish from the drunk actor, who actually ordered the duck confit, take the plaice back to table 10, and set it down before a baffled Blaise. I hold my slightly stooped position for a few seconds without looking at anyone, before I snatch back my hand and stand up with a slight groan, as though to put an end to the episode. I'm a tall man, impressive to look at, so I've heard; slightly stiff, well built, poised. I've got wiry facial hair – a moustache. Once, someone told me that I look a bit like Daniel Plainview. I took that to heart. But it's a half-truth.

The doggedness might be true. The inflexible stoop might be true. But Plainview is more durable than me. He looks more outdoorsy. I've got more of a café vibe. Where he's determined and vengeful, I'm more service-orientated and jumpy.

Niepoort

Conversation is flowing nicely around The Pig's table now. It seems as though they've forgotten my serving blunder. I'm supposed to have a comfortable degree of invisibility; it's in the job description, it comes naturally to me. I'm not expected to push myself into the foreground. I glance at The Pig. He's the gentle type. But he's also a businessman, and that can never be forgotten. In a way, he's always negotiating. With charm and tact, he builds relationships so that he can capitalize on them. I've never understood negotiating. Isn't it just about discussing your way to the best possible terms for yourself? Advanced haggling, in other words? That's a primitive thing to be doing. It would never occur to me to ask for a lower price for something, even if the price was unreasonable. If a seller is brazen enough to be asking for that much, well, he should get it. I'd rather work a bit more to make up for the loss. I'm not going to be the one fishing for a discount. Like some tight-fisted Arab. No, haggling has no place in my culture; we pay full price here.

The Pig gets up. Is he going downstairs, is he going to the toilet? No, rats, he's coming towards me. I fold the napkins as quickly as I can without being sloppy. What does he want now? There are two older women sitting just behind me, whispering away so quietly and feebly that it sounds like whistling. They wheeze a steady stream of half-truths to one another, and one of them is making such sharp S sounds that it's like a scalpel slicing into my eardrums every time she says 'laundress' or 'west side'.

'Excuse me, can I ask you something?' The Pig says gently.

'How can I help?'

'There's something I've been thinking about,' says The Pig. 'That Tom Sellers character, who often sits at the neighbouring table, do you know him? Isn't he some kind of art connoisseur?'

'Could you excuse me for two seconds?' I say, scowling wildly over the heads of the lunch guests. And there, as though on cue, with a comic's timing, the widow of account-ant Knipschild gives me a slight wave indicating that she wants to settle up.

'No, listen here, there's something I want to say,' The Pig says.

'Mr Graham, I'm so sorry, could it wait a moment?' I'm squirming like an adder. 'I have to see to Mrs Knipschild. She's in a hurry. You know, age.'

Age? What am I saying? What is happening?

'Not to worry,' says The Pig, giving me an utterly bourgeois smile, with the proviso that anything can be called bourgeois in this country. Even the slightest hint of deviation from the intended tone is picked up by us highly sensitives. It may be unfair to call The Pig sly, but I can detect a hint of slyness in him now. What does he mean by 'not to worry'?

Sellers? What does he want from Sellers?

Widow Knipschild is sitting, as she often does, with a book to the side of her plate. She reads page after page. Suddenly, two well-tended hands appear, take hold of the plate and move it away. Her eyes remain fixed on the book; from her angle all she can see are the hands coming in from the periphery of her field of vision. The hands take things away. They reach for the glasses and napkin. Those hands are mine. It's me. I make objects and food come and go without being noticed myself.

'I'll be back with the bill in a moment, Mrs Knipschild,' I say.

Widow Knipschild has had the foie gras. She has the foie gras quite often. She might even order two courses. First a terrine, then some fried foie gras. She has apple with it, and that apple should be spiced with star anise. Possibly even a bit of caramel. And before you know it, the goose liver has been washed down with a fortified wine from the pressed grapes of the steep, narrow Douro Valley, and it should say 'Port' on the label. If it doesn't say 'Port' then these drops are not suitable for washing down the liver of the goose. Not for Widow Knipschild.

She's like a razor, or should I say a Shun knife, when it comes to cutting through the culinary, but using bank cards and payment terminals is not her strong point. The chip is upside down, the strip is worn, the code is forgotten, her bluish, witchlike fingers have to rifle through her purse, where she keeps a handwritten note of her codes – and which are, she claims, also written in 'code'. It gives me time to scan the restaurant, and because of my intimate knowledge of distances and placings here, I know that a glance roughly 110 degrees to the left will give me the opportunity to study Child Lady in three-quarter profile from behind. As in, I want to be able to study her without her seeing me. From this angle, Blaise suddenly looks like Child Lady. Maybe it's because I'm straining my eyes. Now both of them resemble The Pig. It's like a magic mirror. Child Lady is abstract now. I blink. They're joking at the table. The Pig's laughter is loud and ringing, and it always drowns out the others', it's the kind of laughter which breeds laughter and keeps the collective laughter balls in the air a little longer. Blaise Engelbert has the rougher, more booming type of laugh that members of the social elite often do. His 'howls of laughter' are like the columns beneath The Pig's architrave, if I can put it like that.

The internet is slow today, and Widow Knipschild waits for the payment to be processed. She uses the time to claw about in her pillbox. Out pops a pill, she takes a tablet. What's it for? Or possibly against?

'Excuse me?'

Her head trembles faintly as she looks up at me. The payment goes through.

'I couldn't have another glass of Niepoort?'

Widow Knipschild's voice has the metallic clang which often takes over elderly ladies' vocal cords.

'Of course,' I say. And this is a bit unfortunate, because her previous glass was actually the last of the Niepoort. In other words, I'll have to go down to the cellar. Why? Because the short-haired, anaemic Vanessa, who is my junior in all respects and who usually goes to the cellar if it's needed, is out for a while.

'Out for a while?' I ask.

'Running an errand,' the Maître D' says. 'She's having her hair cut.'

A haircut? When did the waiters start getting their hair cut during working hours? This is a European restaurant, not a beauty salon. You come to work looking presentable, you leave looking presentable. Never bother the colleagues with your grooming. Of all things, the Maître D' is being generous about Vanessa getting her hair cut.

'The whitest tablecloths get dirty first,' he says.

I'll have to go down to the cellar.

The Cellar

The cellar beneath The Hills is where we keep all our plunder. Everything has to go down there. Access to the cellar is from the street, something which is fairly unusual in Oslo, but which you see quite often in New York, for example, where things are always being heaved down to cellars through hatches in the pavement.

Down in the cellar, there is an intricate shelving system. I don't have much business in the cellar, and have never been to its very deepest parts. Still, I've been in the area closest to the stairs and peered in. I've seen how the shelving system vanishes into the darkness. The Chef has explained in a mumble that further ahead, there's a fork in the central aisle. The walls are curved, and the shelving system, which consists of both open and closed shelves, as well as small drawers, in two tiers, adapts to these curves.

There are also a number of cupboards placed randomly

on top of and next to one another, and cabinets with bev-
elled fronts, divided into smaller cupboards. Parts of the
shelves are covered in metal racks, and the incalculable
level of detail makes it seem more like some kind of elong-
ated aeroplane cockpit than a storeroom. The way they've
utilized the space is unbelievable. The sheer abundance of
surfaces, platforms, drawers and cubbyholes . . .

The shelving system is old. They say that parts of it have
been here since the very beginning. Yes, they say that Benjamin Hill, the founder himself, built the shelves just before
his clothing business went bust. That seems likely. The
drawers and small cabinets are ideal for haberdashery –
buttons, cotton reels, pins and needles, combs – and
hardware – nails, screws, hooks, knobs and so on. They say
that Hill hid down there when overcome by shame between
bouts of drinking and sessions losing dizzying sums at the
poker table; it was down there that he took himself when
everything else seemed impossible. This isn't just drawn
out of thin air; it's a matter of record that Hill was an
apprentice at his uncle's carpentry firm in Windsor around
1830, half a decade before the charmer and dandy in him
emerged and drove him to the exclusive and frivolous
locales of the Norwegian capital.

Luckily, the Niepoort is close to the cellar stairs. I need to
take only a few steps along the left-hand row of shelving
to find the relevant place – a wide and deep, aged, metal
drawer. It's made of forged steel, heavy as lead, yet it moves
easily on smooth runners, and has some kind of velvet

padding inside. The drawer is full of Niepoort, ruby, tawny, Colheita and so on. And some Tokaji, oddly enough. Oh, they're roomy, these drawers. I take out two Niepoorts, but as I try to close the drawer by giving it a hard shove with my hip, I manage to trap my left hand horribly. That bit on the edge, below the little finger (is it the hypothenar eminence? What do you call the *edge* of your hand?). The pain is hellish. I moan loudly and hiss between my teeth, which means I also send a string of drool flying on to my nice waiter's jacket. I manage to get the bottles to the floor without breaking them, press my hand between my thighs and continue to hiss and splutter, because this is absolutely excruciating. I don't dare open my thighs to look. It's impossible to tell whether my hand is crushed, cut or broken, or what the damage is. It hurts so much that it feels like some kind of cruel joke. I can't believe it. I try to walk off the pain. I stagger knock-kneed back and forth between the rows of shelves with my hand clasped between my thighs. I don't go too far down the aisle, because I don't under any circumstances want to go *deeper* into this mouldy cellar. I don't think I've cut myself, it doesn't feel wet, it doesn't feel like there's any blood. I don't want to look. I stand beneath the streets of old Oslo and groan.

I've got a haematoma beneath the skin: a blood blister the size of an unused condom puffs up. It's swelling, and I'm thinking of piercing a hole in it, but I'll have to go and see the Chef for that. I grab the two bottles of Niepoort in my right hand and clamp the injured left one under the opposite armpit. I'll be damned. I flip the cellar trapdoor (steel) shut with my heel, and it makes a terrible noise as it hits the frame (also steel). That's just how it'll have to be. I go round the corner and in through the back door, into the kitchen.

'Can you poke a hole in this?' I say to the Chef, holding up the hand with the blister.

'We'll see to that.'

'It's really about to burst.'

'I'll do it with the oyster knife.'

At the same time, I hear a 'hello' from the swing doors. It's the Maître D', all puffed up, staring. I reply, hurriedly.

'Yes?'

'Vanessa needs a hand,' says the Maître D'.

'Vanessa's back?'

'Yes, she's back. Haircut all done.'

'Ah.'

'Who looks outside, dreams; who looks inside, awakes.'

He continues, 'She needs help. She hasn't served table 13 before.'

'Table 13's arrived?' I say.

'Table 13 has arrived,' says the Maître D'.

'Oh God.'

PART III

Sellers and His Group

Oh dear. Tom Sellers and his group have placed themselves at table 13, right by the bar, two tables away
from table 10, where The Pig sits enthroned with his chosen ones. Table 13 is also my table. This isn't good. Like
The Pig, albeit for radically different reasons (to do with
the aforementioned donations), Sellers has the run of The
Hills as his own 'parlour'. He and his followers usually
come in the evening, when the noise levels are slightly
higher and the morals a little lower, but they're here now,
Sellers, Bratland and Raymond, at 13.47, right in the middle of the day.

He never makes a fuss per se, Sellers. He's a *'gessæl'*, as
they say in the countryside; a scamp, but a cultured one.
Strictly speaking, Sellers is fairly well rooted, but he pos-
sesses that stray, vagabond-esque aura that characterizes
certain people, perhaps fewer and fewer these days, particularly here in the organized north. He's a rascal. The

impression of being a sophisticated scamp that he radiates makes him irresistible to many. Or maybe not irresistible, but appealing. Or maybe not appealing in the sense of being attractive or magnetic, but of being desirable to other, aspiring scamps. The scamp in Sellers gives him an authority in certain environments. He has an aged scamp's face. Sellers has that thick, leathery, George Clooney skin on his face, but he's more worn, greyer and without Clooney's fortunate bone structure. He's not an ugly Clooney; rather, he's got Clooney's skin stretched over a bigger skull. Clooney's skin, but smoke-clogged, boozed up and stretched over a scamp's skull. His hair is starting to turn grey. He looks like Picabia after he'd had a bad night's sleep. He gives off a certain mousiness, even if he is fundamentally 'robust'.

Sellers doesn't radiate the type of personal grooming that otherwise characterizes the clientele at The Hills. He's a handsome man, I want to say that. A bit threadbare and rough around the edges, but serene. Worn. A nerveless face. It's clear that he has 'class', but he's equally shabby. He looks intelligent, and that gives his shabbiness 'bite'. He's a rusty al dente. And then there's the effect of the alcohol. Some people's drunkenness is helpless or foolish. Sellers' drunkenness is perceived as intentional. Challenging. One can interpret Sellers' drunkenness as a critique of other people's sobriety. He positively *basks* in uncomfortable situations. Sellers is someone who likes mischief. Fun is produced all around him. He's almost impossible to knock off his perch. Sellers looks difficult.

Sellers is complex. There's no understanding him. Is he an enigma? He probably is. What does he *want*? you ask yourself. What does he *do*?

'Never will I work, O torrents of flame!' Was that Rimbaud? Sellers doesn't do much, but he carries on; he's proactive in his uselessness. There are plenty of stories about him. The Bar Manager is chock-full of information. She says that the General Manager, M. Hill, who is very obliging to Sellers and his group (think donations), claims that Sellers and his friends belong to a certain *historical* trend, a tradition that values infantile nonsense above all else. The Maître D' disagrees, and argues that Sellers has never been part of any historical trend, quite the opposite, in fact. But the General Manager, according to the Bar Manager, insists that Sellers' endless stream of nonsense actively reflects certain features of the twentieth century's cultural history. The General Manager takes pride in her profession and wants there to be a trace of this cultural history at The Hills, the family business. She wants the story to continue to play out, not to 'evolve' but to be repeated indefinitely, so that everything that wasn't ridiculed fully during the first round, from 1914 onwards, can be ridiculed and derailed again and again, in the same way.

According to M. Hill, the great ridiculing that began in the early twentieth century – The Hills' golden era – was never completed. It'll never be completed, which means that a short cut through time is needed, so that the positions begun but never finished (a.k.a. the ridiculing) can be picked up anew and repeated. These are positions that will always be misunderstood, and which must therefore be played out again, so that the misunderstanding can be maintained for ever, since misunderstandings are often more effective in the here and now than as history. The Hills is one of the few places where there is room for that. Or that's what the General Manager pompously claims, anyway.

Sellers is dour, it's true, but the Maître D' insists that dourness of itself doesn't make him heir to the Dadaist throne. Sellers, Raymond and Bratland carry on with their tenacious, aimless, stagnant nonsense, but that's all it is. Being drunk and disgusting isn't an art form, the Maître D' says. No, on the contrary. The bitter attacks that Sellers and his group direct at everyone around them are weak, schmuckish. The only thing they've worked out, if you ask the Maître D' – and this is if we're following the General Manager's line of thought, via the Bar Manager – is the classic question of whether they should have fun in the here and now, in life, or save the gratification of desire until after the revolution. Since we're no longer in a position to see 'revolution' on the horizon, Sellers, Bratland and Raymond have fun – 'fun' – right here and now. They've long known, the General Manager argues, that we're moving about in a representation, a social, political, economic, existential representation, which, as an increasing number realize, has become a sheer parody of what was once an 'existence'; the situation, the conditions, have moved so far beyond a joke, a pure jest, that all suitable responses have stopped being suitable. Mockery is the only thing left. The General Manager claims that Sellers once told her that his aim is to prevent the day from being nothing but twenty-four hours of wasted time. Well, even the Maître D' agrees with that. But that's where the agreement comes to an end.

It might look like Sellers is smoking in here, but he isn't. The smoking ban came into force years ago, and even an avant-gardist like him smokes outside now. Sellers 'acts' like he's smoking, he looks like some kind of '20s photo, or, to be more precise: he looks like a photo from 1923. I look like a photo from 1890, or at least I would if it wasn't for Child Lady sitting right behind me being wildly contemporary. The Pig looks like a photo from 1984. Sellers' slender friend, Bratland, looks like a gnome. His face is at once young and old. I've never liked this Bratland. Eyes too close together. I have quite an appreciation for Sellers and Raymond, despite all their nonsense, but I can do without Bratland. I'm a bit jumpy around Sellers, but he is dashing. Bratland is foul. He always has a foul expression on his face. A snake-like smile. Dead, mackerel eyes. Always a remark. Bratland will be bald in three seconds. He's not much to look at. To be more precise, and keep the mood in the early twentieth century: he actually looks like the Surrealist Jacques Vaché. He's got the ratty, Conan O'Brien-like face of Vaché placed on the high shoulders of Bernie Sanders. And with bad teeth.

If an obscure name is mentioned around table 13, the otherwise talkative Bratland goes quiet. Then he goes to the toilet, while Sellers and Raymond continue to talk, and when he comes back, he suddenly has plenty to contribute. He's been trawling the internet from the toilet seat, he's been swotting up. A crowd-sourced genius emerges from the WC. He always uses the internet to paper over his grotesque incompetence.

Raymond, that great beluga of a third man in Sellers' group, is the opposite. He looks like a hobo, with a greasy fringe. His face is a mask of hairy old leather with two holes and a ravine, but what comes from this ravine, his ravine of a mouth, is pure gold. Raymond has internalized knowledge, he isn't a toilet-seat academic like Bratland. Raymond has a scar under his mouth which makes him look slightly affected, slightly sore, as though his chin were constantly rippling with tears. Raymond has a sweaty charisma and is well liked. He is extremely capable. I don't know what a genius looks like, but I can recognize one when I see it.

The Situation

Have the festivities gone full circle? Sellers and company are slow in their movements. They're by no means loud or screeching, the way people usually are after, say, a liquid lunch. Instead, they seem to be settling into that slump when the party has gone on for almost twenty-four hours and has become a test of endurance, a marathon, some kind of job. Sellers' group seems more concentrated than festive. They're finding their sea legs. Sellers' gestures are sluggish and his gaze is slow. I hold the hand with the blood blister behind my back and come to the aid of the newly hired, short-haired Vanessa as she wanders about with the stack of menus clutched to her chest. I know Sellers. Or rather, I know him as well as I know all the other regulars here. I've been seeing him for years. He's been seeing me for years. I know plenty about him. He knows nothing about me.

'Would you like to see the menu?'

Tom Sellers rubs his thighs. He rubs his avant-garde thighs. It's hard to tell whether he's an alcoholic, as such, but the rubbing could seem addict-esque. A bit needy. He's always drunk. They decide on a round of Birra Morettis, all but Bratland, who wants white wine.

'The house white?' I ask.

'No.'

'Would you like to see the wine menu?'

'Rather not.'

'I see.'

'You don't have a Californian Chardonnay? Californian.'

'Of course.'

'Then I'll have a huge glass of that.'

'Anything to eat?'

There's something about keeping up the formalities even with a boisterous type like Sellers. We all know that they are going to eat, but we also know that it's *comme il faut* to ask rather than assume this, so I fulfil the job of asking, staring and waiting. I can do that. The exchange of glances ends with a nod from Sellers, and I take my hand and my blister over to the bar, where I find the Morettis, previously brewed in Udine but now owned by Heineken, isn't that right, and the Chardonnay which has been grown, picked and crushed in sun-drenched California. My blister throbs and stings. I need to finish serving the drinks before the Chef and I get to work with the oyster knife. Puncturing stuff, poking holes, penetrating – these are never at the top of my list. But what are the alternatives? The blister is about to burst.

Sellers starts singing quietly:

> 'E ricomincerà
> Come da un rendez-vous'

Many years ago, we had a jukebox here, just like in the Cuneo in ugly Hamburg, which played Paolo Conte and other Italian classics with plenty of echo. 'Gli Impermeabili', and so on. I think Sellers misses it.

'Please, Sellers,' Bratland says.

'Keep out of it,' says Raymond.

The atmosphere around the three is a strange mix of refreshing and unpleasant. Can you imagine a smell that's both fresh and rotten? Once, I had to change a bunch of lilies that had gone off in their vase. Our florist had let it happen. They didn't smell of lilies any more, they smelled like crap. The strange thing was that the lilies were still in bloom, but their stalks had withered. A sweet smell of decay mixed with the fragrance of the flowers. Lilies have a truly disturbing scent, especially if you don't cut off the small stamen, or whatever it is that's inside the flower and stinks. Our florist annoys me. He lets that happen sometimes. No one from Sellers' group looks up when I serve them their drinks. I turn my left hand inwards, like a claw, to avoid showing the blister. He's an observant guy, Sellers. Not rude, but sometimes he'll comment on small things that embarrass you. What am I saying? They embarrass *me*. I can't speak for others. He's the intelligent type, someone who always sees more than he says.

I hide the blister, I don't want any questions about it. It was unfortunate that it happened. It was no one's fault. I can't point the finger at Widow Knipschild for sending me down to the cellar. Widow Knipschild! Damn it. I glance over to her table, and there she is, with an empty glass, looking straight at me. Her old eyes are staring, the colourless eyeballs searching me and asking, no, wondering what happened to her Niepoort and why I'm prioritizing these youngish (really middle-aged), woozy men. Widow Knipschild's poor eyes. Just imagine everything they've seen. Imagine all the tears that have spilled from them. They've had their fill, those eyes, throughout their long life, of staring and crying. And here they are, let down again. The last thing her tired eyes need is to register yet another disappointment.

I can feel my chest contracting. My breathing becomes shallow. It often does when I've got too much on my plate. Widow Knipschild is sitting there with her eyeballs, she even lifts a bony hand in the air to catch my attention. Her hand shakes so slowly that it looks like she's waving. And as though that waving, bony hand wasn't enough, The Pig also turns his head and nods to me. What does he want now? What does he want, this Pig, who has everything? I signal that I'll be with him in two seconds. Vanessa is still circling Sellers' table. The blister is pulsing. I hurry into the kitchen.

* * *

'Can you lance it?'
  'What?'
  'The blister.'
  'Let's see.'
He takes my wrist in an excessively hard grip and breathes a long, slow breath through his squashed nose. He studies my hand, the way a blacksmith would study another blacksmith's work, for example, or the way a sushi chef would study a piece of fish by turning it and peering at it from different angles. I don't know why he wants to seem so 'professional' – he's a chef, not a surgeon. To him, to whom God gives office, He gives also understanding. But the Chef's office isn't the puncturing of blisters. He takes the oyster knife from the magnetic strip (it's mounted beneath the bench, not above it) and presses down firmly into the blister. The stream of blood must be finer than a strand of hair. Like an acupuncture needle, inexplicably thin. I don't think the Chef sees it to begin with – his eyes aren't the best – and the spray has time to hit the chest of his white chef's jacket before moving upwards, across his collar, up his neck, towards his face. Suddenly, it's on his cheek. Now he reacts. Maybe he's equipped with particularly sensitive nerve endings on the skin beneath his eyes. *Eeeeiii*, he bellows in disgust, with

97

some kind of *euhhh/aaah* sound, meaning his bellow becomes an odd mix of a word and a shout, a noise with no specific meaning, almost like retching, a sound produced by the body when language falls away. He grimaces, or smiles, and it looks like he has a tear of blood on his cheek, which he quickly wipes away with the arm of his jacket. He wraps one of the tea towels around my hand before he presses on the blister and empties the blood into the material (linen).

The question is how loud was his shout? Did I hear a moment's pause in the clink of cutlery and buzz of voices out in the restaurant? It was a bizarre sound he produced, the Chef. A shout and a retching sound that was also like a bleat from the mouth of a sheep. Muzzle. The snout of a sheep? That's how he bleated. Did they hear it? I try to 'sigh' but can't get the air all the way in, and I produce a strained hiss instead of the deep housewife's sigh I wanted to make. The blister is empty and has become a pale flap of skin instead of a potent, full blister.

'What do we do now?' I say.

'You'll have to put a piece of gauze on it, otherwise you'll tear the skin.'

'Do we have any gauze?'

'Maybe a bit. In the wardrobe.'

I have to get going. The Pig is waiting, Widow Knipschild's glass is still empty. She needs her Niepoort. She'll get so much Niepoort. And The Pig, does he want to see the dessert menu, or does he want to tease and agitate me with hypothetical questions about Sellers and rare works of art? I squeeze past the Chef over to the old yellow medicine cabinet in the wardrobe area, and apply a double dressing over the flap of skin. I'm terrible at applying dressings, and it ends up lopsided and loose. I wrap what little gauze there is around my hand. It really is an amateurish attempt. What kind of provocations is he up to, The Pig? With the Niepoort in my good hand, I go out through the swing doors, back into the restaurant, back to the guests. The Pig turns to me and holds my gaze. Child Lady also looks up. Widow Knipschild stares at me with those grey eyeballs, waiting, hoping for the bottle of Niepoort. I go to her first. I hold the Niepoort up high, almost level with my breastbone, so that there's no doubt in Widow Knipschild's mind over what is about to happen.

It's generous, the serving I give her. I don't stop. I fill the glass to the brim.

'Oh, thank you, thank you,' she says.

Then The Pig.

'You're busy?' he says.

I recognize it well, around my right eye, the tension. I don't know what my right eye has to do with my emotional state, but it's always around my right eye that it appears. 'It' appears. What does? Distaste. Anxiety. *Tension*.

'How was the food?' I ask.

'Wonderful,' says The Pig.

I would like to look in a mirror to check how visible the tension around my right eye is. I can feel a marked tenderness around my right eye now. 'And the mushrooms did the job?' I say to Child Lady.

She giggles. 'That depends which job they were supposed to do.'

Blaise chuckles.

Which job were the mushrooms supposed to do? Who knows. They were supposed to do the mushroom job, I guess. Now is not the time to try to be funny. Unhappiness makes reliable consumers, Edgar often says. That also applies to Child Lady. She smiles 'childishly', but she's not fooling me. How many squadrons of riot police are needed for her to smile like a child? I make use of my only defence, the standard phrases.

'Can I tempt you with anything sweet?'

My left hand is firmly behind my back to avoid waving the gauze bandage in the guests' faces. A dressing placed over a wound isn't exactly what you want to see while you're tucking into Arctic char, tart or bouillabaisse. The only problem is that my back is turned to the watchful Sellers and company while I talk to The Pig, so my hand is on show, so to speak, no matter which way I turn. I can almost feel Sellers and his group's eyes boring into the compress and the loose skin flap beneath it, while I try to tend to The Pig. Sellers is so conflict-oriented. I turn to him.

'Everything OK out in the kitchen?' Sellers says, ambiguously.

'Oh yes.'

'Just let us know if you need any help.'

'That won't be necessary,' I say.

'Oh well,' says Sellers. 'Just let us know.'

'Anything else to drink?' I ask.

'Have you lost weight?'

Sometimes, as I'm serving, or taking orders, I become aware of my own stoop. There is nothing to be admired about a stoop, but there can, seen from a particular 'angle', be something about stooping which fits well with being a waiter. There's plenty of leaning forward in this job. I'm bent over Sellers' table right now. I stoop more when the situation gets heavy.

'I've been the same weight since I was nineteen,' I say.

'Good age. Nineteen. The evenings. The oomph,' Sellers says.

It's just a case of getting away. I've signalled that Vanessa should take the dessert and coffee orders from The Pig's table. What will it be? Vanessa manages to mess it up. She can't keep track of a single cortado, a double espresso, a double cortado and a single Americano. She has to ask again. Were both cortados doubles? No, just the one. And the Americanos? Single? Yes. And a double espresso, no?

'This shouldn't be so difficult,' says Blaise. He says it in a slightly prissy manner, too. He snaps slightly, there's a sting to what he says. A sting which is heard a bit too far away. The observant Sellers and his table are *very* sensitive to snapping and prissiness. They might be endlessly indifferent to their own appearance, to the unease they consistently bring with them, but other people's snapping, stinging – particularly if it is directed 'downwards, from above', as they say – well, that's going to be noticed. A snap of the kind Blaise serves up to Vanessa is seen as 'crude' by Sellers and his entourage, I know that. I know them well. Blaise is, as described, particularly well turned out. 'Crudeness' becomes proportionally more crude depending on how well groomed the purveyor of the crudeness is. As a result, the crudeness he casts out becomes even more piggish in Sellers' and Bratland's ears. There will be consequences, I fear.

Sellers would never attack with anything but his vocabulary. He waves Vanessa over and calmly reels off what he wants. Vanessa nods despairingly. It's a lot to remember. She goes to the bar and immediately returns with a number of coffees, plus a stack of hors d'oeuvres on a serving tray. It almost seems like she won't be able to carry it. She approaches Sellers first and puts down two of the coffees, but Sellers corrects her and she takes them back, not without effort, then carries the whole overladen tray to The Pig's table and sets them out, one by one, along with seven bowls of fennel salami. The Pig's company is silent while she works. And once the slightly dazed Vanessa is finished, there are nine double Americanos and one Turkish coffee on table 10, in addition to all the salami. Vanessa studies the table. What has she done?

'Johansen!' Sellers shouts.

The playing stops.

'*Schweigt stille, plaudert nicht!*'

Johansen fires up Bach's Coffee Cantata.

*

No blows are struck, of course, but some feathers are ruf-fled. Blaise gets up and goes over to Sellers' table. Bratland, belligerent as he is, gets up to meet Blaise. They stand there, uneasily close to one another. Bratland is a good ten centimetres shorter than Blaise, but Blaise is seven miles ahead when it comes to attire.

'Is this your coffee order?' says Blaise.

'I do order coffee from time to time,' says Bratland.

'Is it his?' Blaise points to Sellers.

'What's wrong with coffee?' says Bratland.

'What?'

'The tycoon's out for a stroll?'

'What's going on?' says Blaise.

'Manners. They apply to you too. You're in a restaurant.'

'Come again?'

Blaise holds out his arms and glances around as though searching for confirmation of the absurd nature of what is coming out of Bratland. He doesn't get a thing. Perplexed, Vanessa begins to move coffees and fennel salami from The Pig's table back to Sellers'. The Maître D' and I approach the disputants from different directions, and he asks them to kindly calm down a little. Bratland doesn't pay him any heed, but Blaise yields, gentlemanly as he is. He takes a step back. I place a hand between Bratland's shoulders, to pacify him, but he shrugs it off like a teenager.

'Shame on you!' he says, pointing a finger at Blaise.

The Maître D' takes Blaise by the upper arm and places his other hand on the back of his polished neck. He steers the fragrant man back to The Pig's table. Will Bratland back down now? Uh-oh, he grabs a piece of salami from one of the bowls of hors d'oeuvres. But before he has time to throw it at Blaise or Child Lady, to eat it or whatever it is he's planning to do, Sellers swats his hand, making him drop it. I shout a firm 'Hey!' The fennel salami flies in a gentle arc, straight into the glass of the lovely little Isa Genzken assemblage hanging to the right of table 15, before falling behind the almost monstrous radiator which stands there with its countless layers of peeling glossy paint. The Maître D' reacts strongly, with a jolt, a spasm.

'Watch the Genzken!' he says, pointing firmly at the artwork.

The fennel salami leaves a greasy mark on the glass. Sellers squints. He's enjoying this. It looks like he's trying to focus on the grease on the Genzken. He's trying to get the fat in focus, to take it in.

Nez

'Clean the Genzken,' the Maître D' says, his voice thick.

I go straight into the kitchen to get the Windolene. The Chef looks up at me from his flambéing – he probably heard the commotion out there, but he doesn't ask. He never asks. He has an ability, the Chef, to know exactly what's going on in the restaurant without being out there himself. And while I'm wiping, The Pig comes over and asks whether the picture is OK. Sure, it's fine. It's just grease. And then he's at it again. He wants to talk.

'It was a bit unfortunate,' he says, 'this episode.' Because it was Sellers he wanted me to introduce him to. It so happens that Blaise has come across an artwork they need someone knowledgeable to look at.

'And it should be someone who, how to put it,' says The Pig, 'will give it a look under the counter.' Sellers is competent, so they've heard.

'That may be,' I say dismissively.

'I don't want to run this past the management,' says The Pig. 'It would be best if you, being a waiter, could introduce me to Mr Sellers,' adds The Pig. 'Completely without obligation.'

I decline.

'It's way beyond my duties,' I say. 'I don't want to get mixed up in this. Take it up with the General Manager (M. Hill).'

'But you don't understand,' says The Pig. It transpires that Blaise has a real gem at home (one of Hans Holbein the Younger's small portrait sketches, not the most famous – a small pale one – but it's a Holbein all the same, one of the Tudor drawings, no more, no less), and he needs to get a conversation about it under way, with someone suitably discreet. Something The Pig assumes Sellers is. Blaise is thinking about donating it.

'No, thanks,' I say again. Holbein? 'No, no.' I say it louder. 'You'll have to do that yourself, Mr Graham. I don't want to get mixed up in this.'

'But I need an introduction,' says The Pig. The Pig is old-school, he demands an introduction.

'Then you'll have to introduce yourself,' I say, surprised at my own directness.

With that, The Pig leaves. Blaise struts off through the curtain with a plutocrat's ease. Child Lady remains seated. I'm still 'double-checking' that the Genzken is grease-free.

The Maître D' is in the middle of the room. He has paused, as rigid as a statue. The Maître D's face, which, even to begin with, has that drinker's glow, that unhealthy hue, has turned an even deeper shade after what has just occurred. I think Child Lady should leave. She should have the decency to leave the establishment and allow the dust to settle. Instead, she hangs around like a bacillus. She moves, that's true, but only to a different table, to one of the smaller marble-tops by the entrance. I wish she was gone. I wish she'd never set her fancy feet in here. How can we push her out?

Sellers looks absent, with a thousand-yard stare, seemingly unaffected by the unpleasantries which just took place. His group orders a new round of Morettis, all but Bratland, who insists on that terrible Californian Chardonnay. It's gone four, almost half past. Here comes Edgar, holding the curtain to one side for Anna, who slips in beneath his arm, radiantly cheerful, with her sweet child's face. Can she sense the toxic atmosphere? Should I escort her chaste, innocent soul right back out?

'Hi!' she says to me.

Edgar is also in a mood.

'Do your homework, Anna,' he says.

Anna, without complaint, pulls out her books and starts *immediately*, no hesitation. It truly is inspiring to see how she knuckles down without beating about the bush. All that back and forth, what's it good for? I hold the bandaged hand close to my left thigh.

'Dad says you're good at the piano.'

'Not at all,' I say. 'I've never played the piano. What homework do you have?'

'Maths.'

'What kind of maths?'

'Geometry.'

'Oh, that's easy.'

'Yeah . . . but the compass wobbles when I try to draw circles. It's loose.'

'Let's see.'

I catch a slight whiff of pencil case as she pulls it out. The mix of pencils and rubbers has the distinct smell of school. So they're still doing it. Pencils and rubbers. It won't last. Nothing does. I take the compass; it is fairly slack, and a loose compass joint is, as everyone knows, frustrating. Grotesque, even. A compass is anything but a compass when it's loose.

'I'll ask the Chef to tighten it,' I say.

The Chef nods mutely in the kitchen and tightens the compass screw with the tip of his most expensive Henckels knife before turning back to the careful frying of a beef tournedos. I don't smell the Chef's cooking any more, but I know that this dish in particular has an exceptional aroma. But God help me if I haven't forgotten to add both the tournedos and the coq au vin to the board of specials. I grab a piece of chalk from the bowl behind the spool of butcher's twine. As I walk through the restaurant, Bratland shouts, 'Rach!' loudly, which means that old Johansen switches to Rachmaninov up on the mezzanine, the internal balcony, and Piano Concerto No. 3 it is, Brat-land's favourite. I take the Morettis and the Chardonnay and let them land, as quickly as three tits on a bird table, beneath the noses of Bratland, Raymond and Sellers. Then I hand the compass to Anna.

'What's going on?' says Edgar.

'Going on?' I raise an eyebrow and try to hold my face steady. I try dragging it in the opposite direction to the downward pull caused by the strain.

'You look a bit harassed.'

'We had a slight situation.'

'A *situation*?'

'A slight situation.'

'I see.'

Edgar doesn't have much patience for my non-communicative tendencies. He shrugs. Anna is busy drawing perfect circles with her newly tightened com-pass. From the corner of my eye, I can see that Child Lady has flagged down the inexperienced Vanessa. She spends a while talking to her – this might be more than an order. What is she planting in Vanessa now? What seeds, which ideas?

'Anna's worked out what she wants to be,' says Edgar.

'Oh yeah?' I say. 'A geometricist?'

'There's no such thing as a geometricist,' says Anna.

'What do you want to be, then?'

'A perfumist.'

'A perfumist?'

'Yes.'

'There's no such thing as a perfumist,' I say.

'I want to work in a perfume shop.'

'You want to be a perfume-shop employee?'

'Yes.'

'That's something different to a perfumist.'

'OK, a perfume-shop employee, then.'

'If there is such a thing as a perfumist, it must be someone who *makes* perfume,' I say.

'They're called "perfumers",' says Edgar.

'Yes, of course.'

'Or *nez*. French for nose. Someone with a good sense of smell,' says Edgar.

'I don't want to be a *nez*,' says Anna. 'I want to work in a perfume shop.'

'Why's that?'

'The people working there are so cheerful.'

'That's true,' says Edgar. 'They are.'

'You want to be cheerful?' I say.

'Yes,' says Anna, 'that's what happens when you work in a perfume shop.'

'I suppose it is.'

Edgar explains that they were in a perfume shop the other day. It had struck him (them) how incredibly positive the woman working there was.

'She was so unbelievably cheerful,' he says, and Anna agrees. 'You should sell something which smells good and makes people cheerful,' says Edgar. Anna nods. 'We talked about it afterwards,' says Edgar, 'about how cheerful and nice she was. The same with the orthodontist. The woman behind the counter is so boundlessly cheerful. You should fit braces to teeth so they become straight and inviting. You should do the job really well and no more than that, but no less either. You should be in a position to send people home with straight teeth or smelling nice. And then you could head off at the weekend to a forest cabin or some other nice place as fast as your feet can carry you. Ideally every weekend. And on top of that, you should focus intensely on holidays and celebrations. Immerse yourself in the Christmas preparations. Put up decorations without restraint. Master Christmas. Go crazy with Easter eggs and decorative birch twigs, when the time comes. I think that's a source of happiness. Seriously,' says Edgar.

'What did you buy at the perfume shop?' I ask.

Edgar is evasive.

'Something for a friend.'

'Well, what do you know,' I say.

'Musk,' says Anna.

'Musk?'

I know who all of Edgar's female friends are. He isn't buying musk for any of them, that much is certain. This is interesting. The musk is left hanging in the air alongside everything else that's already hanging in the air. There's so much hanging in the air. Is there ever nothing hanging in the air?

'Who is this friend?'

'One you don't know about.'

Anna places one arm of the compass in front of the other and makes it walk like a thin, stiff-legged fellow across the sheet of paper in her notebook, in a way not dissimilar to how I trudge around. I've started to trudge with age. If I have to do a U-turn, I take a number of supporting side steps rather than doing one firm, solid turn.

Sellers waves to me. He isn't any more sober, nor is he more drunk, he's *level*, I suppose you could say. He wants food.

'What do you two want?' I say to Edgar and Anna. 'I have to move on.'

'I want lasagne,' says Anna.

'I'll have the butter sole,' says Edgar.

'The butter sole,' I repeat.

'Can you add some extra capers?'

'Extra capers on the butter sole.'

'It's a bit strange, maybe, but I once had a spoonful of date jam on the side. Can you arrange that?'

'Dates with the butter sole, of course.'

'Dates,' says Anna.

'Do you want dates?'

'No, dates are . . .' She waves her hand in front of her nose and pulls a face.

'Ask him to overcook the mushrooms a bit,' says Edgar.

'Crispy?'

'Borderline crispy.'

'And the butter browned.'

'Yes, browned butter.'

'What would you like to drink, Anna?'

'Apple juice.'

'And a glass for you?'

'I think I'll allow myself a glass of the one from the Loire . . .' says Edgar.

'Savennières Clos—'

'No, Coulée . . .'

'Coulée it is, then.'

Sauceboat

Every bird sings with its own beak, the Maître D' says. This applies not least to Raymond. He draws out his vowels when he speaks. When he comes to order food, these long vowels blend with the notes being produced by the fat fingers of old Johansen playing away up on the mezzanine. Old Johansen has drifted into a Rachmaninov lullaby. It's beautiful, but it's also fairly slow and, to be honest, deeply tedious. A strange choice for this time of day. The woozy Raymond orders an entrecôte with the tune tinkling away in the background. He has a deep voice, Raymond. He sounds like a baritone. His order becomes some kind of miniature musical. He wants the entrecôte done medium rare, and for the sauceboat to be 'compleeeeetely' full of Béarnaise.

'To the brim,' he says, 'but I only need half a portion of the onion marmalade.'

'Wonderful,' I say.

On the whole, says Edgar, *mastering* speech is primarily a case of ignoring the embarrassing untruths and inaccuracies we deliver in every sentence. Raymond doesn't struggle with that. His order of entrecôte and a full-to-the-brim sauceboat, which he delivers in harmony with the music, is a joy to the auricles. The ears. To us waiters, who might find ourselves dealing with all kinds of stuttering during orders, it's nice, from time to time, to be served a decent order, if I can put it like that.

The same can't be said of Bratland. His language doesn't add up; the syntax creaks and groans.

'If you wait two minutes, I'll write up the day's specials on the board,' I say.

'Why can't you just say them?' Bratland asks.

'I like to write them down,' I say. I bring out the three-legged stool, climb up on to it and stretch as far as I can. The board is high up – everyone needs to be able to see it. As I reach the 'd' in 'tournedos', the chalk makes a shrieking sound which causes Bratland to swear. He digs one finger into his ear. As I continue with 'coq au vin', the 'i' screeches and Bratland swears again.

'You're tearing my favourite music to shreds with your racket,' he says. I ignore him and draw a firm line between the food and wine recommendations, the chalk squealing so loudly that Bratland huffs and puffs again.

'Like stabbing a screwdriver in your brain,' he mumbles. I put away the stool and point to the board. Bratland squints. 'I can't read that scrawl,' he says.

I explain that it says 'tournedos' and 'coq au vin', but

the truth is that I've written 'turdonés' and 'couq au vergin'.

'I don't want that, anyway,' says Bratland.

'Wonderful,' I say. Sellers orders confit de canard, as usual.

'The petits pois are still ripening?' he asks rhetorically.

'They're far from full maturity.'

'You know, I want them basically *unripe*.'

'They're absolutely verging on unripe.'

'And could you ask the Chef to add a tiny splash of veal gravy to the thyme gravy?'

'Of course,' I say.

The dinner guests start to arrive. Edgar's and Anna's food is ready, and I take it out to them. Anna claps her hands with genuine enthusiasm as I place the lasagne on the table.

She is probably in the last six months of having such adorable outbursts. They peter out and disappear for good after turning ten, don't they? Everything adorable gets phased out and replaced by something different. Some un-enchanting trait. What is the opposite of delightful? Despicable. Adult. The Chef's lasagne is fantastic, served to Anna in a small earthenware dish, and still sizzling.

'It's red hot,' I say.

'I know.' Anna smiles.

'They're starting to get lively over there,' says Edgar.

'Who?' Anna asks.

'Around that table over there,' says Edgar, nodding to Sellers' alcoholic milieu.

'What's wrong with them?' says Anna.

'They've drunk a lot of beers,' I say.

'How does that work for you?' says Edgar.

'What?'

'Them carrying on like that?'

'It's who they are,' I say.

'I'm just asking,' says Edgar, but he knows that Sellers is given free rein in here.

'I have to move on.'

'Yeah, look, they want their food now,' Edgar says, making a 'grandiose' gesture towards Sellers and the group.

I serve everything as ordered, with the exception of the sauceboat for Raymond, which not only do I not fill to the brim, but in which there is a provocatively small amount of Béarnaise. Raymond wrings his hands as I place it next to his plate.

'Goodness me,' he says with that singing, deep voice. Without a murmur, I take the sauceboat back to the kitchen and fill it all the way to the brim, as requested.

'Is this some kind of performance?' he asks when I come back.

'I beg your pardon?' I say.

'Are you making these mistakes on purpose?'

'What are these shenanigans?' Bratland butts in.

I move my head, neither a nod nor a shake. It's more an

unwelcome jerk, a tic. It feels like I'm jolting awake after nodding off for a second. Bratland sneezes, which sounds like someone has slapped his face.

'You're a good waiter,' says Raymond. 'You know full well what I asked for. I asked for the sauceboat to be full to the brim. Then you come out here with a nigh on empty 'boat. Next, you fill it to the brim and act like nothing has happened.'

'Don't you start too,' Sellers says, either to Raymond or to me, I'm not sure.

'The 'boat is full now,' I say at the precise moment Raymond says, 'It's not me stirring things up.'

'Why don't you drop it,' says Sellers.

'Why take the cursed 'boat for a walk?' says Raymond.

'Forget the 'boat,' Sellers orders.

'It's forgotten,' Raymond says, holding up his hands in surrender.

Sellers steers a large chunk of duck thigh to his mouth. He chews with deliberation. 'Not much veal in this sauce,' he says.

'I asked the Chef to add a little.'

'I think he forgot.'

'He usually pays attention,' I say.

'Then you'll have to drill him again,' says Sellers.

'The Chef is his own man.'

'Ah, is he cooking for freedom in there?' says Sellers.

'It's not a question of freedom *for*, but freedom *from*,' I say.

'Well, aren't we combative today,' says Sellers.

I clap my hands together and walk through the restaurant, over to the bar, in a wide arc, where I collect a disappointing Chardonnay, return to table 13 and fill Bratland's glass to the brim without asking him if he wants a top-up. He responds by taking a slurp so large that his eyes snap back in his head.

Critique of the Female Body

Child Lady gets up from the marble-top by the entrance and walks over to Sellers' rather alcoholic avant-gardist table. The Bar Manager, the Maître D' and I all observe this. What business does she have with Sellers? She exchanges a few words with the intoxicated man and introduces herself with the same choreography she used on The Pig, and, to an extent, on me. She never creates anything new, I think; she just re-creates herself.

Eyebrows are further raised when she tips forward and gives Sellers what can only be described as a bear hug. All of her grace is released into his open arms. He wraps them around her and squeezes. Then he holds her in place, with an adult hand on the back of her head, in a prolonged, solid *knus*, as they say in Danish, the language of Europe's most dishonest people.

The Bar Manager leans in and whispers that it's astounding that she suits these men as well as she does the others.

'Spending time with both The Pig and Sellers on the same day is an artful move. It's to do with something deeper than grace,' she says. 'When you look at this woman, you might suspect that there is no beautiful surface without terrible depths beneath it.'

'But does she know them?'

'We'll see,' says the Bar Manager. She's in a good place now.

The embrace ends, and Child Lady's hands remain on Sellers' shoulders as they hold one another's gaze like old friends. They hug again. Then she giggles. She turns to the two other drunks in Sellers' group and sits down between them, on a chair which she most boldly pulls from table 11. All I can do is set another place.

'Thank you, but I've just eaten,' she says to me. Oh yes? Have the mushrooms I arranged been lost in oblivion? The order I served her under an hour ago, has it been forgotten? Is she trying to cover up this double manoeuvre, this overlapping, by feigning ignorance, suddenly sitting here at Sellers' table? With brisk movements, I unmake the place setting for her. I pick up the cutlery, napkin and glass in reverse order, as though I'm being played backwards. It's impossible not to exhibit my bandaged hand, the covered blister. Maybe it's my imagination, but I feel like Child Lady, Sellers and not least the razor-sharp Raymond are all looking at it.

'I'll take a glass of Pinot Noir,' Child Lady says.

'*Jawohl*,' I say firmly.

I spin around in confusion and run the crumber over a couple of tables that have just left. What am I saying? This is madness. She wants Pinot Noir now? What does that mean vis-à-vis The Pig's white burgundy? Increasingly, it takes so little for something to unsettle me. What is happening? This constant feeling that everything is going wrong. I am blurting out German words which belong neither here nor there.

It's Child Lady, I'm sure of it. This thing about her age: how she looks disproportionately young, and yet seems so aged and experienced that she appears fatigued and slightly worn. How old is she? She's porno-old. She wears a number of rings on her fingers, indicating capital at its most serious. One of them sits on the knuckle of her middle finger, glittering and quivering like only diamonds can. It's almost baroque, but she makes it work with the rest of her get-up, which is a combination of expensive design and high-street tat. I can see both Miu Miu and Dries Van Noten, along with a slightly weak Balenciaga, and a surprising pair of shoes. They're relatively clumpy and colourful, with thick tongues, like old skate shoes. But they are surely new editions. Airwalks, maybe? What an idea.

Child Lady looks like a heavily made-up kid, though not tastelessly so. When I arrive with the Pinot Noir and lean forward with my slight stoop, I think that it might be age that makes her child's face seem more defined, sharper, like she's not so heavily made up after all. I let the wineglass approach the table without a sound and think that I mustn't turn towards her now. I'm not crazy – I can't turn around and stare her in the face. It's just not the done thing. But I'm interested in this notion of make-up versus age. I'm reluctant to admit it, but standing here, with the glass still making its way towards the table, I get the urge to turn my head to the left and give Child Lady's face a good stare.

I arc over her right shoulder and let the glass silently meet the covered table top. I can feel her warmth, I'm so close. She gives off a faint scent of . . . the 1980s. Almost masculine. What is that smell? I keep hold of the stem of the glass for a moment longer while I lean over her, in my handsome waiter's jacket, in my waiter's trousers, in my worn, but still solid and well-cared-for shoes. That's how I'm standing, with my dry hair and my so-called nervy face, which I always try to tighten or hide behind my moustache. That's how I'm standing, thinking that it would be interesting to inspect the relationship between make-up and age on Child Lady's face. So, I turn and stare. She looks back. The distance between the tips of our noses – hers Greek, mine prominent – is the breadth of two Swedish sourdough loaves, no more. I should never have arranged this 'meeting'. She parts her lips and teeth, pulls her tongue down from the palate with a click and says, '*Jawohl*.'

I slowly loosen my grip on the elegant stem, the glass filled with a light, good wine made from the Côte-d'Or's big grapes, Pinot Noir, and pull my hand away. I place it next to the bandaged claw behind my back and try to stand up straight. My lower back protests; I pull myself up like a cadet, with a quiet grunt and a stern face, until I end up in some kind of vertical position. There's nothing I can say to that.

Nabokov had a funny approach to interviews, Edgar has told me: he insisted on writing down his answers first, and sending them to the journalist, who could then work out the questions. Here's the answer: you tell me. And the question? What the hell are you going to do with yourself after this blunder?

Of the opportunities for withdrawing I have here at The Hills, every one is time-limited. I can go into the kitchen to seek refuge with the Chef, but he's probably in an irritable mood as usual. I can yap a bit with the regulars – I'm allowed to spend more time on them than the others. I can go down to the cellar to fetch things, but that's something I tend to avoid, as I've already said. I often feel chaotic down there. I've already done a loop with the crumber. I charge over to Edgar and Anna.

'Everything OK here?' I say formally.

'Yes,' says Anna. She has eaten most of her lasagne.

'Slow going over there?' says Edgar.

'It is what it is,' I say.

'Yes . . . and that latest addition complicated things, I suppose.'

'What?'

'Well, do you know who she is?'

What is Edgar suggesting? Does he know her? I have a sinking feeling.

'Excuse me?'

'Her, the girl.'

Her, the girl? Is he suddenly a specialist in Child Lady? I stare at him but can't read his tight face. God forbid. The perfume. Was the perfume for her? It was musk she smelled of. What kind of charade is Edgar playing? Does he have an interest in Child Lady? Is he speaking with a forked tongue? It's years since he announced he was keeping his distance from the opposite sex. His distaste. But what's going on now? He once told me that, though it might sound unfair and immature, the female body had lost its appeal for him.

'Here comes a critique of the female body,' Edgar had said. That was what he called it. A critique of the female body. I nodded and smiled, the way I always do.

'On the one hand,' he said, 'and this is nothing new: the mediated, impeccably maintained and sculpted female body hasn't just made the ordinary, standard, common, everyday body that the vast majority of women possess superfluous. The mediated female body has made the day-to-day female body unbearable to be close to. The everyday body has no appeal because the mediated female body is constantly forced upon us. Fair enough. But on the other hand, the seemingly perfect female body – the one left as an object of desire now that the everyday body is over – is linked to the vilest form of monetary turnover, to such a degree that it ceases to be attractive. It's a body which, if you stare at it, stares back. But it's the eyes of the hawker you're looking at. The tanned woman's body, with hundreds of thousands of squats in its resumé, and millions of followers on social media platforms, is the hawker's face mask. He has pulled that woman's skin over his skull and is staring back at you like some kind of Leatherface.'

Anna had been there that time, too, but she was quite small, maybe in the first or second year of school. She had an exercise book with her. Edgar couldn't have said all this in front of her now.

'All I see is the sly hawker,' Edgar continued. 'And the hawker's plan doesn't make me lustful, let me tell you. Excuse me, but isn't it time these women covered themselves up a bit? This exhibition of meat and flesh can't go on. Whenever the sun comes out, and we're going to the shop or out for a coffee, they force us to look at their hideous arse cheeks hanging out of their too-short denim shorts. Why do I have to have these sad cheeks in my field of vision, making me stare? I see cleavage. Cover yourselves up. I see a navel. Cover it up. We don't want to see your navel. We never want to see thighs. The sight of a stupid, stupid female arse is the last thing we need to see, now, in these times. It's sad for you. It's sad for us. It's like we're reading an ironic epilogue. The female body is a freed slave who has come back to tyrannize her former owner. See here: everyone has strings up their bum cracks. The female body has become synonymous with the hawker's business interests.'

That's how Edgar talked. But now he has met Child Lady and calls her 'her, the girl'; he's changed his tune.

PART IV

Sleep

Every morning, I'm stupid enough to check my phone when I wake up. Today, still lying in bed, I had to relate to a video comparing the agile jumps of animals with those of athletes. An automated, five-necked lute playing a tune on itself with some kind of robotic fingers. A teenager who made a functioning Luger out of straws. A clip of a drunk man (the Baltics? Russia?) who manages to stumble *into* a rubbish truck and disappear. Two unfaithful women being stoned in the so-called Middle East. A Brazilian boy refusing to eat chicken wings because he's seen the film *Chicken Run*. A debate about the Californian drought and Nestlé. An article about Baudelaire's hashish consumption. A swing bridge in India decorated with thousands of grotesque little cloth dolls. A sad Ford Mondeo advert. A Sami teenager's singing making a female foreign minister (Spanish? Polish?) cry. Because of this, I'm already wrecked by the time I get to The Hills to start the morning shift.

Old Johansen's liver-spotted hands dance across the piano keys on the mezzanine. I thought the Maître D' had forbidden him from playing it, but he is actually playing Pachelbel's canon for three violins and basso continuo, his Canon in D major. The piece doesn't sound great on the grand piano. Old Johansen has, however, sharpened it up a little, making it more difficult to recognize, which is possibly why he's getting away with it. Pachelbel's canon for piano, however flabby it might be, is still preferable to a lot of other things. Rap music, for example.

I've attached the *Zeitungsspanners* to the spines of the newspapers and started serving cappuccinos, espressos, Americanos and one freshly baked croissant after another. In between making espressos, the Bar Manager is adjusting an uncomfortable ring. She rubs her finger, the ringless one. Representatives of the adult world of conversation and commerce come in one by one, ordering what they want to put in their mouths, which, as a rule, is something coffee-based, followed by rolls and pastries. Who said that the concept of *living well* was a craze for times of crisis? Was it Balzac? Was it Cioran? If this isn't a time of crisis, I don't know what is. Sometimes, when I overhear what is being said at the tables, I find it's not really possible to distinguish between genuine statements and parody. I have real trouble discerning sincerity from satire. The farce of everyday life seeps in, even here at The Hills where we try to keep it at bay through rigid routines.

You can probably assume that businessmen, civil servants and lawyers don't parody their own world over their morning coffee, but it certainly seems like it.

I opened the bandage today, at the crack of dawn. The blister looks horrendous. The skin is pale and dead and loose. I wrapped it back up in the same bandage.

The Bar Manager has tried to talk to me about how things unfolded last night three times now, but I wriggle out of it. I fetch the coffees she places on the counter, and carry them over to the tables. I won't let myself be fooled, I don't want to talk about yesterday. I've got enough to think about, I don't need to speculate about Sellers and Child Lady, and, worse, Edgar and Child Lady. I'm like a shuttle service with coffees in my hands. As long as the Bar Manager places coffees on the counter, she won't get any conversation about yesterday out of me.

She just stood there all evening anyway, glaring passively while I ran around like a headless chicken, serving and making sure Anna was OK while Edgar went over to Sellers' table and strutted his stuff, with handshakes and laughter. Why was Edgar being so crazily impulsive? You don't go over to other people's tables like that, like some autograph hunter, you just don't. He was even asked to sit down, between Child Lady and Raymond. I had to serve him while he sat there on his throne. He let me carry over one Moretti after another. It behoved me to serve. Behooved? Anna had immersed herself in her book over at the other table, drinking a hot chocolate for what seemed to me – and probably also to her – like an eternity.

Edgar had given her a fantasy book – not exactly ambitious, in other words. I asked Anna about the plot, but didn't really get it. A group of teenagers were being kept as 'tear slaves' in a dystopian, futuristic dictatorship. Thanks to a serious shortage of H^2O, 'tears' were a resource, and certain poor, unfree creatures (emotionally unbalanced teens) were forced to cry in a factory. No, that can't be right. That seems too thin, even for fantasy. Even for fantasy? What do I know about fantasy?

'Doesn't Anna have school tomorrow?' I eventually had to ask Edgar. It was almost quarter to eleven. Anna was sitting there at her table, and Edgar, cackling and smiling between Child Lady and Raymond, at another. He took the floor every now and again, I saw. He went on about this and that, and had the entire table listening. The clock struck quarter past eleven before he pulled himself together and left, dragging an overtired Anna with him. Indefensibly late for a schoolchild, you could say. I left shortly after. Sellers, Child Lady, Bratland and Raymond continued their bacchanal. Yes, that's the word the Bar Manager chooses to use – their bacchanal continued until the restaurant closed, well into the night. Child Lady was there until the very end, says the Bar Manager, in a tête-à-tête with Sellers.

'They were talking about cars,' she says.

'That can't be right,' I say.

'Yes, they were completely absorbed in a conversation about automobiles, the car industry, different models of Ferraris. It sounded like autism for two. "The old 250

Lusso is a masterpiece," Sellers said. "Can you call Pinin-farina anything but a master?" Child Lady replied.'

All this while I slept.

And, what do you know. Here comes Child Lady – so early – through the curtain, pushing it to one side. Is it her? It's only quarter past seven. I'm not sure. It's like her. Yes, it is her. Isn't it? She looks like herself. She looks like a thousand others. But it is her, it has to be her. There's nothing special about Child Lady, and in a way that's her beauty. Fresh as the morning dew, wrinkle-free, feature-less, beautiful. She looks rested. She sits at the bar, right in front of the Bar Manager, who will be making a firm men-tal note of that, if I know her right. What's her order? Quadruple espresso. Another quadruple espresso. Does she ever sleep? As Edgar often says, sleep is good. Sleep is an uncompromising break from the theft of time that the hawker subjects us to. Edgar likes to sleep. The major-ity of seemingly irreducible necessities in life – food, drink, friendship, desire – have been rediscovered in financial forms, so to speak. Sleep is a human need and a 'dead' interval which can't immediately be colonized or placed under the hawker's yoke, Edgar often says, slightly clumsily, jabbing with his index finger. In that sense, sleep remains an anomaly, an unknown territory for the hawker. Despite all the research in the field, sleep contin-ues to frustrate the hawker and to render his strategies for exploiting or reshaping it impossible, Edgar says. It's not bed manufacturers I'm talking about here. Nor the psychoanalysts, with their dream interpretation. The fascinating truth is that nothing of financial value can, as yet, be extracted from sleep itself.

But doesn't Child Lady sleep? She just keeps coming back like an itch or the flu or the taxman. I'm all for predictability and repetition, but the routine of being exposed to her every day . . . I'm not sure I can handle it. Her continued presence makes everything else wobbly. She's wearing crisp, fresh clothes. No kinks in her hair. Not a hint of bags under her eyes. She looks productive. She sits there, sipping her quadruple espresso, just a short time after participating in the bacchanal around Sellers' table. Yes, I'm calling it a bacchanal too, even if it wasn't, strictly speaking, a 'sumptuous celebration of the grape'. Sellers' bacchanal is more a celebration of *the flaky*, it seems to me. A celebration of ongoing, persistent procrastination, time-wasting, with tormenting idleness the consequence. Flakiness. An indulgence of inactivity and inept behaviour. How can Child Lady be so energetic after taking part in that all night?

She reaches for an object. Sometimes, for brief moments, language eludes me. One word or another dissolves completely, and I am unable to find it when I need it. Right now, I can't think of the word for the object lying on the counter. I panic. As I lose the ability to attach words to things, like now with this object of Child Lady's, I become one great big eye, an enormous retina. What's it called? Aphasia? Can one develop aphasia without having had a stroke, without a tumour on the brain or some other damage?

The object is colourful. She grasps it and retrieves something, fishes it out – a telephone – which she then swipes with an elegant finger and raises to her lovely ear, an ear decorated with a large, glittering earring. It must be a diamond.

Thirteen Missed Calls

'I'm at The Hills,' I hear her say. 'No, no . . . Yes, I'm here now . . .'

She clears her throat with sounds like a small engine.

'Definitely! I'm not kidding.'

With that, she giggles quietly and turns away, as though she wants to hide her laughter from the Bar Manager, and possibly also from me, standing here like a statue. The Bar Manager has placed a glass of water next to Child Lady's coffee. The water remains untouched, but the espresso goes straight down. Now she rubs her phone as she sips her quadruple. She rubs and rubs the glass with her index and middle fingers, and stares at the screen. She leans forward, bends over it, shielding the screen, you could say. I collect a plate and a cup from the now-empty table 3, where a City lawyer was just eating. As I set the cup and saucer on the bar, I cast a long glance, as it's known, at Child Lady's screen, but can see precious little. Is she on social media? Probably. As long as I can't see the screen properly, I don't know a thing about who she interacts with, even though she is sitting right in front of me.

And not just that. I honestly can't know whether she's reading or looking at pictures, either. I don't know if she's political, an activist, if she pays her bills, if she works, has sex, watches films, talks to her parents, goes to college, is buying clothes or furniture or a car. It's impossible to know. The way she hunches over the screen is and will be the same, regardless. The square centimetres of the screen have, in a sense, taken on a similar function to banknotes – the absolute translator of all things, I've thought, via Edgar. Work, leisure, pictures, relationships, knowledge, nonsense, text, bullying and drudgery, buying and exchanging, production and unrestrained consumption, birds and fish, endless inventiveness and excessive control, desire and systems. Everything can be translated into money, and all this can be translated again to play out on the screen.

The majority of 'things' become styled and trimmed down to fit the screen, just like all 'things' are styled and reworked so that they can be turned into money, in one way or another. Banknotes and the screen are related. The screen is the banknote's window. The screen is the hawker's window. That's probably it. The hawker stares back up at you from the screen. He probably does. Especially at Edgar. Child Lady raises her head before I manage to compose myself. I'm rubbing my hands on a kitchen towel embroidered with the restaurant emblem, bleary-eyed, probably, and staring at her for no good reason. She stares back. For a moment, I see the hawker staring at me, the way he stares out from the screen. Now I see Child Lady. Now the hawker's awful face is visible again. And now I see Child Lady's immaculate face once more, and all I can do is fold the towel into a long rectangle which I lift up and bring down against the bar like a short bull whip, or baton. It makes a nice crack, and it looks like some kind of habit, hopefully – a ritual, a waiter's standard practice, something 'French', something to symbolize a full stop, the transition from one duty to another.

I spin around and immediately start going over the tables with the ceaseless crumber. I *slash* crumbs and croissant flakes away, imagining that my sweeping looks experienced, but also feeling enormously stooped and idiotic. Child Lady jumped a little when I whipped the embroidered tea towel against the bar. She looked at me. Imagine the number of waiters and coachmen (now taxi drivers) who have quietly been forgotten by history. Imagine the number of men who have vanished into waiting work or driving, in Europe, over the years. The eternal coachman. The eternal waiter. There has been plenty of driving. There has been plenty of dishing out food and quenching thirst.

Child Lady gives me a wave, and I go over. There's a distinct smell around her, which I maintain is musk. Unfortunately, I slept on one cheek last night, meaning I have a vertical crease from my eye down to the corner of my mouth. I must have been in the same position all night, because the crease won't go away, and makes me look considerably older than I am.

'Excuse me,' she says.

I lean forward to suggest 'attention' – yes, I'm actually leaning against the counter, and my hand is resting right next to her clutch bag. 'Clutch' was the word I was looking for earlier, for that object of hers.

'Do you know what Mr Sellers said to me yesterday?' she asks.

'Mr Sellers?'

'Yes, Mr Sellers.'

'No.'

'He said that I'm an obsessive thought.'

'What?' I say.

Child Lady giggles, she raises her hand to her mouth. I am – as I often am – left in the same position, unmoving, like poultry, fowl, because I don't understand. A new giggle forces its way out. It looks like she's trying to make a 'poor attempt' to 'hide' the fact that she is 'giggling' from me. I'm standing there, with my right hand on the counter and the bandaged blister behind my back. Even when she giggles, Child Lady is at work, I think.

'Don't touch the bag,' she says.

I realize my hand is resting too close to this clutch of hers, and pull it back as though from a hot baking tray.

'And do you know what Edgar said to me?' she asks.

'Edgar?'

'Yes, you know. Edgar, your friend.'

'Yes, I . . .' I say.

'Do you know what he said?'

They're on first-name terms. It's one thing that she's in

circulation, that she moves from The Pig's table to Sellers', but that Edgar is now part of this circulation, this 'scene', is disturbing. Yes, there, I said it. Disturbing. How long has this been going on? Edgar played up for Sellers' table, that was easy to see. He turned it on for Child Lady. Stood up straight. Gesticulated, moved a lot, virile.

'Don't you want to hear?'

'Just a moment,' I say, moving backwards like a cray-fish. I have to get away.

The Chef is busy chopping in the kitchen. What's being chopped? Isn't the early morning for poaching eggs? His chopping is firm, it feels like he's whacking my cranium. There's an old butcher's block behind him. I stand to one side of it. The block is at least fifty centimetres thick, and equipped with an iron belt around the middle. The ceiling above the block, or the chopper, as the Chef calls it, is just as black as the vaults above his gas hob. It's like a black abyss. There's an old-fashioned garlic press on top of the block, grey and well used, its plunger section almost black. Where does Child Lady know Edgar from? I don't understand. There is a carton of twenty or thirty cherry tomatoes, and I push them into the garlic press one by one, squeezing and making some kind of tomato mush – ketchup – from the tomatoes, which runs straight on to the floor. What is the musk around Child Lady? Is it Edgar's musk? Does he carry it around with him? Doesn't musk mean 'testicle' in Sanskrit? What is Edgar up to? Has he given her *musk*?

'What are you doing?' says the Chef.

'Me?' I say.

'Why are you making a mess? What have you done to my tomatoes?'

'I'll clean it up.'

I move my head clumsily from right to left in search of a cloth.

'And you need to answer your phone,' says the Chef.

'What?'

'Your phone. It's been ringing non-stop in your locker.'

My phone never rings 'non-stop'. As a rule, there are zero missed calls at the end of a working day. I never check my phone at work. There's nothing in my life worth ringing 'non-stop' for. Repeated calls this early in the morning can only mean that something has gone wrong.

'I don't check my phone when I'm working,' I say.

'So I have to listen to it all day? I need the tomatoes.'

'Not at all,' I say. 'Is it OK with you if I check it?'

'That's what I'm asking you to do.'

'We're not allowed to use our phones. We'll have to tell the Maître D' it's an emergency.'

'An emergency?'

'It probably is.'

'Just check your phone.'

'I'll get the tomatoes.'

I go into the staff wardrobe corner and pull the ungodly device from the pocket of my all-weather jacket. Edgar has called thirteen times. That's a bit much. Did something else happen yesterday? Was he too drunk when he left with Anna? Is someone hurt? Why am I asking myself?

Wouldn't it be better to ring him? Can I allow myself to call him back?

'Can I allow myself to call back?' I ask the Chef.

'Allow yourself.'

Edgar answers, he *takes the call* in a second, with a huff and a clearing of the throat, and explains that he has to travel to Copenhagen on 'urgent business' – he wonders whether Anna can come down to The Hills after school.

'The trip is work related,' he says. 'She can just sit there.'

'What?'

'She's used to it. A soft drink. You don't have to keep her entertained.'

'No, no.'

'Just give her a bit of food.'

I see myself as highly conflict-averse, but if I don't want my nerves to be the end of me, I need to toughen up and explain that it's stressful for me to be responsible for Anna while I'm working. Edgar has no sympathy for that.

'Your job's pure routine,' he says. 'Isn't that the whole point? Put food in front of the girl and chat for ten minutes, and the job's done. Give her a Coke. She doesn't need special treatment. She'll do her homework and read. It's easy. We're talking about a child. One child is nothing, two are like ten, so they say. Her meal will have to be on credit, that's the only difference.'

'Food *on credit*?'

'I won't be back late. I'll pick her up in good time.'

'In good time like yesterday?' I ask with a bitter undertone.

'Hey, watch it.' Edgar's tone becomes sharp. 'How bad was it yesterday? Am I not allowed to let my hair down once in a while? Am I not a single parent, do I not stay at home, night after night alone in my flat, year in and year out? Hasn't my mother died? Do I have anyone else to help me? Is Anna's mother a pill-popping wreck or not? Aren't you a friend? Is it so much to ask?'

'No, of course it's not,' I reply. 'It's not too much to ask. When you put it like that. You can send Anna over after school.' Why the onslaught? He is attacking me with his child.

Romanesco

The Chef's back is hunched and rounded.

'I need tomatoes. You have to fetch more tomatoes,' he says.

'What?'

'Four minutes.'

'Where are they?'

'The cellar.'

So here I am again, standing by the cellar hatch, feeling my nerve endings twitching, and taking in the fact that Sigurd the Crusader tramped around these same square metres 885 years ago. This is where he walked, the son of a king's mistress and barely forty years old. He had already been king for twenty-six years, taciturn, not kind, but good to his friends, and faithful. And here I am, in the same place, ready to open the cellar hatch and go down to fetch stalks of tomatoes. Yes, the distance between what happened when Sigurd walked here and what is happening right now has to be seen as infinite. An infinite distance, seen from a human point of view, but a distance equal to zero from a geographic perspective. He stood *here*, Sigurd, in Oslo, on the cusp of death, after an utterly epic life. A phenomenal life. After having sabred down Muslims on the edge of Europe. 'Sabred' might be the wrong word in this context – he stabbed them with a sword, at least, possibly with a bearded axe.

I can't find the right key for the padlock; it's difficult to hold the heavy chain in my bandaged hand while I fiddle with the Chef's enormous bunch of keys. Why is it so huge? The padlock and chain are bitingly cold, and my hand goes numb. My breathing is getting shallow. I produce brief bursts of frost smoke. The hatch is as heavy as lead, the stairs are steep and perilous, with steps worn down by use. But why is the light on? The bulb hanging in the first corridor is burning brightly. I'm bent over at the bottom of the stairs. The back of my head is touching the ceiling, it's so low. And I thought The Hills had high ceilings. I glare diagonally downwards, towards where the fork in the aisle is supposed to be. Is there someone down here?

'Hello?'

The countless drawers, cabinets and shutters disappear in the obscurity of the central corridor, before the much-discussed fork appears. The tomatoes are kept to the left, along with the other fruit, in the drawer section beside what looks like a control panel. Tomatoes are classed as vegetables in many Norwegian homes, but botanically speaking they're fruits, with large, juicy and, not least, nutritious seeds. Using my right hand, I fumble my way to the fork in the aisle, I press the blistered hand against my thigh. Below, at knee-height, beneath a 'fore-drawer', you're supposed to be able to turn on the light in the next section, according to the Chef. It's not easy. What is a fore-drawer? My fingers run beneath a series of five drawers with sloping fronts. Could these be 'fore-drawers'? All I can feel is soil or soot, something dry, powdery. Beyond these, I reach behind something resembling a bureau. I'm down on my knees now, and then before I've managed to reach the other side of it, I'm on both knees and an elbow, thanks to my injured hand. I pull on a small knob and the light comes on. I look at the panel above me. Dashboard? Are these fuses? It can't be the air conditioning? The wall where the tomatoes and other fruit are kept is divided into a number of new drawer sections. A couple of stalks are sticking out.

'Yes, hello,' I hear behind me, while I'm still on all fours.

Jittery and bent-backed, I manage to crawl into a half-standing position and come face to face with the Maître D'. What's he doing down here?

'What are you doing down here?' I ask.

'What am I doing down here?'

The Maître D's big face is almost entirely without expression.

'How's it going?'

'How is it going? What do you mean?' he says.

'No . . . of course.'

'We need the small pewter plates for the pats of butter.'

'Aha,' I say, making a small OK sign with my thumb and index finger. The pewter plates he's talking about are the sweetest little things. They're Danish, and they have a banner engraved around the edge, as well as the previous owner's initials, dated 1789, as a matter of fact. There's an anchor and a gull in a circle stamped on the back. They've been in the Hills family's possession, incredibly, since three-quarters of a century before the restaurant opened. These Danish plates have a diameter of eight centimetres. It would be an exaggeration to say that the bags beneath the Maître D's eyes were as big as the pewter plates, but they are big, those bags, so it doesn't seem an unreasonable comparison.

'Well . . . hunger knows no friend but its feeder,' he says with a clearing of the throat which sends the unmistakable scent of Kremlyovskaya vodka up my nose. Then he turns, after another brief stare, and crawls up the awfully steep stairs.

'You'll have to get up.'

The idea that vodka doesn't give away a secret drinker is only half true, I think to myself.

The vegetables are on the opposite wall, some of them in open drawers, and between the cauliflower and broccoli, beneath an overgrown and fairly ugly turnip, are three impressive romanescos. I like romanesco. Romanesco is something I've always liked. Not the taste, but the appearance. Not that it's all that original, but I've always been fascinated by the romanesco's fractal shape. It's almost too much. It's not necessarily tasteful, visually, the romanesco. You can't make a judgement on its tastefulness if it's naturally spectacular, can you? I feel a deep, childish joy whenever I see a romanesco. Has Anna ever seen a romanesco? Probably not. I decide to take one up, so she can see it later. If she's bored. After her homework is done and the fantasy has been read, when the conversation with me dries up. I will keep her busy. I will keep her entertained. I will dig a moat around her with my routines.

The Florist

It's eight in the morning, I'm exhausted already and it's Friday, which means the florist is blooming by the back door, to be glib about it. The florist does his floristry a couple of times a week, and always on Fridays, so that the flower arrangements are fresh and crisp for the weekend. I've got my arms full of tomatoes and the romanesco, and I ask him to go in. The florist is the least florist-like man you can imagine: he's no lover of gossip, and he doesn't exhibit any unconventional preferences. He doesn't have the glasses, hairdo, scarves or challengingly cut clothes you would expect. He's young and looks more like an artisan from the Balkans than a florist. But he takes his floristry all the more seriously for it, and offers both flower arrangement and design. As well as selling them, he even grows some of the flowers himself, which means that most aspects of the flower trade are covered by his business. He leaves the actual floristics, however, alone.

I asked him about it once and was given a brief, dismissive answer. I know he has a fundamentally ikebana philosophy, adapted to a traditional, European customer base. Sure enough, he steers clear of contemporary European arrangements, and focuses instead on asymmetry, negative space, dramatic pauses and silly counterpoints. I nod tensely at the door stopper to hint that he should use it while he's bringing the bouquets of flowers in and out of the algae-green Duplo van parked in The Hills' own parking space. As though he doesn't know that already, about the door stopper. As though he hasn't been here before. As though he doesn't bring flowers to The Hills twice a week. My lack of tact does complicate situations.

'Did I ask for romanesco?' asks the Chef.

'Not at all,' I say.

'Then what's this?'

'Romanesco.'

The Chef gives me a dead look.

'I brought it up to show Anna. I thought it might be fun.'

'Anna . . .'

'Yeah, she's coming here after school. She has to stay for a while.'

'Ah.'

'Edgar, her father, is in Copenhagen on business.'

'. . .'

'So she has to stay here a while.'

'. . .'

'I thought the romanesco could be something.'

If I have the ability to drag a conversation out, the Chef is the grandmaster of driving it into a ditch. We stand there for a second, staring at one another and breathing, him through his flat nose, me through my moustachioed mouth. He places the tomatoes on a chopping board and turns his back to me. I return to the restaurant. The twitching in my head is out of time with the steps my legs are taking, like a fowl again, a peacock perhaps. And as I lock eyes with Child Lady, I feel the damn romanesco weighing heavily in my right hand. Why haven't I put it down? Why have I brought a cauliflower out into the restaurant? Child Lady looks at the vegetable and then up at me. She waves and I, still bird-like in my movements, can't see any other possibility than to skip/waddle/strut over with the cauliflower in one hand and the blister/flap in the other. She places her phone on the counter, screen up. I wish I had another face to give you, another visage to present, I think. I would have liked to give you the face I had, say, twelve to fourteen years ago. But that face is gone. It doesn't exist any more. Like so many other things. The only face I have is this one. A mug exposed to considerable wear and tear. I can feel it, the damage, the age, when she, decay-free, ageless, stares at it, my face.

'That's some vegetable,' she says.

'Yes . . .'

'Is it a . . . ?'

'A kind of cauliflower.'

'Yes.' She smiles.

'*Romanesco*, it's called. You can taste that it's related to broccoli.'

'Oh really?'

'Yes.'

'. . .'

'And look at this,' I say, lifting the vegetable to her face.

'My word.'

'Yeah, maybe you can see that it's really intricate.'

'Yes, wow.'

'You could imagine Benoit Mandelbrot drawing it,' I say, followed by a 'heh' which is a bit too loud; it sounds like a cough, a clearing of the throat.

'. . .'

'I like this kind of complex or impossible visuality,' I continue, now out of control.

'Such bottomless visualities.'

I'm holding the romanesco with straight fingers, like a small skull, studying it through narrowed eyes, when I hear myself blurt out the following train of thought:

'Think how nice it was in the old Europe, not even that far back in time, when, for example, you might step through a door and up a staircase, and find M. C. Escher cutting his impossible geometric figures on to woodblocks with the greatest of accuracy. So pleasant. He carved absurd and impossible perspectives into his wooden blocks, with the focus of a scientist, and then he made those into beautiful woodcuts. Enjoyable for him to make. Beautiful for us to look at. Things aren't like that any more. It's no longer possible for us to go to the market in Nuremberg and see

Albrecht Dürer and his wife Agnes, née Frey, at the stall she set up next to the fruit and vegetable traders, to sell her husband's prints. The childless Dürer couple went to fairs in Leipzig and Frankfurt and offered divinely inspired prints to the everyman at a reasonable price. No epic genius sells prints on that square any more. You can forget it. Now, it's all doner kebabs and broken-phone-screen repairmen everywhere. Poor Europe. You can get your phone fixed, that much is certain.'

Child Lady is listening. Is she taking it in? I'm floundering.

'It's healthy,' I say now. 'Antioxidants are important.' And isn't that the hallmark of the moron? People who talk about things they have no idea about always talk about antioxidants. 'Antioxidants protect against the body's production of free radicals,' I say now. 'They're important for preventing cancer, among other things. Too many free radicals can damage our cells. You find antioxidants in rosehips and walnuts. In sour cherries and sunflower seeds. Blueberries. And tea. And chocolate! Did you know that?'

'No, I didn't,' says Child Lady.

'Maybe you know what I'm getting at here?'

'No, I'm not sure I do.'

'Well, vegetables are also full of antioxidants. Red cabbage and kale. And maybe broccoli in particular. And who's broccoli's neighbour?' She points to the cauliflower. 'Exactly! The romanesco.'

This is a full-on crisis. I'm left standing with the vegetable in my hand, and with my lips shaped like the mouth of a bottle for a few seconds before, in a panic, I shout at the florist who has just come out of the kitchen with a huge bouquet of lilies in his arms.

'Hey!'

The florist stops. I place the cauliflower on the counter.

'Can you cut off the stamens so the lilies don't start smelling like manure after two days?'

'Of course . . .'

'Good. Don't put it off, please.'

'OK.'

'And you have to *pinch* them off with your fingers, ideally with paper in between. They stain horribly.'

'I know that,' the florist says with a puzzled face.

I've pitched my voice too high, but I can't give in now, and drag it out a little more.

'*Good.*'

'Could I have the bill?' says Child Lady. Her smoothness makes her difficult to read. If she's disappointed, offended, if she's trying to get away in panic, or if she just wants the bill, it's impossible to say. Her face is like an unplugged flat screen, a so-called smart TV without a power supply. She allows her peepholes to cling to me, with their almost bluish whites, until I force out a matter-of-fact, reserved, concise, professional, firm, desperate 'of course' and top that 'of course' with a nod so severe that a lock of hair falls forward on to my forehead. I must look like a clown. With one hand outstretched, resembling a Heil Hitler more than anything else, I shout to the Bar Manager that there's a request to pay at this end of the bar.

'There's a request to pay' are the actual words I use. The Bar Manager places the bill on a little plate which I carry from the till over to Child Lady. The plate is from Rörstrand, I know that.

'The bill for a quadruple espresso presented on a small faience plate,' I say, letting the plate land gently, like a little bird, in front of her.

'A what plate?' Child Lady says.

'Faience.'

'Which is?'

'*Fayance.*'

'. . .'

'It's earthenware. Originally from Faenza. The factories in Delft tried to copy Chinese porcelain – white with blue detailing, you know. Faience became very popular.'

'Ceramics?'

'Yes, you could say that. They've been making faience at Rörstrand since the 1700s. Here in Norway, Egersunds Fayancefabrik have been at it for over a hundred years. We've got a lot of Egersund in the cellar.'

'I'm learning a lot today.'

'But the majority of items from Egersund aren't faience.'

'No?'

'They're stoneware.'

'OK.'

'They're in the cellar.'

'In the cellar?'

'We've got a complex and deep cellar, right under here.'

What am I doing?

Child Lady pulls an impressive wad of cash from her clutch bag while she studies the bill which is resting, with a discreet crease, on the faience plate. There's nothing proportionate about the wad of cash and the price of the quadruple espresso. But Child Lady still has to get them – the cash and the espresso – to communicate somehow.

'You're not interested in hearing what Edgar said yesterday, then,' she says without looking at me.

What should I say to that? She uses her breath and the movement of her tongue to hoot out his name – 'Edgar' – again.

'Edgar has never actually been in the cellar beneath here, under The Hills,' I say. I pick up the romanesco and weigh it in my hand, letting it bounce up and down.

'Never,' I repeat.

'No?'

'No. Never.' I place the vegetable on the counter, and turn it over so that the very tip of it is pointing at Child Lady.

'But would he . . .'

'You know that the Norwegian word for waiter comes from the German *kellner*, which really means *cellar master* – derived from the Latin *cellarius*?'

'No, that's news to me.'

'Well, then.'

She looks up and gives me another smile. If you really want to talk about dental arches, the prime specimen is right here, in Child Lady's mouth. Everything has to be straightened nowadays, I often think, but you can clearly see that correction and straightening have something going for them here, unless it's natural after all, which is no less spectacular.

'That means you're the cellar master, then.'

'I mean, in principle, no. I'm upstairs, well, but . . .'

'Since you're a *kellner* and everything.'

'No, I mean, it's an old term.'

'*Cellar door*,' she says, placing far too large a banknote on the plate.

'What?'

'The most beautiful words in the English language, wasn't that it? *Slide down my cellar door . . .*'

'. . .'

'You know, the children's song.'

'I'll just get your change,' I say. 'Excellent.'

To my horror, she doesn't leave this time either, but sits down at the marble-topped table over by the curtain. What is she? A moray eel lying rigidly in wait by the entrance to the hole?

Old Johansen

We know that too little sleep is bad for a school-child. We see a clear relationship between a lack of sleep and underperformance. They even said so on the radio this morning. They see such things, the people looking for them. We'll also see it in Anna later. When is she coming again? Four? Five? She didn't get much sleep last night, thanks to Edgar's eagerness to press himself on Sellers and his group. We'll see a tired, slightly worn-out Anna when she comes in with her oversized school bag on those slim, bony shoulders, six to eight hours from now. How can they send her off with so many books? She must have to walk with her back bent at almost 45 degrees just so that she doesn't tip over and end up like an upside-down tortoise or beetle. Poor child. Poor, innocent Anna.

Old Johansen is playing tunes, and they're sad, melan-choly. Are they expressive of *the wretch*? The poor beggar? The bloke with the beggar's staff? Is old Johansen on the mezzanine a wretch? He probably is. He began with Pachelbel this morning, and it's been going steadily downhill ever since. It's rare for the Maître D' to allow Johansen to drape such a mournful cloak of music over the restaurant. We can't let him build up (down) to Anna's entrance like this.

What follows is something I've never done before in all my time here at The Hills: I decide to twist my body up the wrought-iron spiral staircase, on to the mezzanine, up to old Johansen. It's quite an effort to climb that staircase. How does old Johansen even manage it? He's as round as a barrel. I've never thought about it before, but he's always up there already when I get to work. I've never seen him climbing the stairs. Have I seen him go down them? No. He's there when I leave, too. I *twist* up the stairs. From the top step, where I have to stand with my neck completely bent because of the low ceiling, I can see his shirt-clad back, divided by his antiquated braces with leather loops and buttonholes into a large, black X (he probably chose these X-shaped braces over the Y-shaped ones because of his width; a hefty man like old Johansen needs two anchoring points on the back of his trousers).

'Johansen, what shift are you actually working?'

Old Johansen lifts his chin up and slightly to the side, he doesn't jump at all, as though there are constantly people coming up on to the mezzanine, behind his back, asking unexpected questions.

'Pardon?'

'What shift are you working, Johansen?'

'The same shift I've always worked.'

He's sitting on a double piano stool, a high-quality so-called duet stool, with two separate and adjustable seats, again because of his girth, I'm assuming. The stool has a knob on either side, one for each seat, and the cushions are covered in first-class velvet in deep burgundy, almost oxblood. The actual body of the stool is made from heavily varnished beech, and there is a music stand to the right. And this comes as something of a surprise: beneath the heels of Johansen's polished shoes is a pedal extender, an old-fashioned pedal footrest. So he's shorter than I thought, in relation to his width. Old Johansen is practically round.

'Hey, Johansen . . .' I say.

'You're welcome,' says Johansen.

(You're welcome? Have I received something? What have I been given?)

'You know that the Maître D' thinks Pachelbel's canon is a tad too melancholic? Since you started the morning with it, you've entered territory that's even more gloomy. Could you lighten it up a bit?'

'Pachelbel's canon is in D major.'

'OK, but can you just make it a bit less melancholic?'

'It is what it is. I can't make it any less melancholic. I don't know what you mean,' Johansen says while he continues to produce smooth, unalloyed melancholy with all ten fingers.

'We've been asked whether you would be so kind as to lighten the mood a little.'

Is Johansen a part of the mezzanine? The relationship between his body width and the spiral staircase is one thing. Another is the piles of notebooks and papers surrounding the piano. All kinds of printed matter and musical literature, it looks like, are stacked up against the walls. The arches of the vault begin no more than a metre and a half above the mezzanine floor, but this metre and a half is more or less covered in these piles. Furthermore, there are several stacks of plates, all different heights. I can see flat dining plates for solid food, deep soup bowls for liquid meals, and several serving plates, in addition to one stack of side plates after another. Several of them are the Egersund faience that I went on about to Child Lady. Isn't the Maître D' constantly looking for these? There are piles of knives, forks and spoons on the top plate of each stack, all soiled with food; it looks like Johansen has been stacking and collecting for a long time. The floor is covered in everything from bouquet wineglasses to fine crystal champagne flutes, all over the place, many of them have forks and other, smaller, basic pieces of cutlery sticking up out of them. I can see a crab spoon peeping up from a finger bowl, also crystal, along with a set of snail tongs, four three-pronged fish forks and, believe it or not, the finest caviar spade we have. Not far from Johansen's pedals, there is a pair of grape scissors on top of a pan for venison, plus a handful of gourmet spoons and the handsome game service inherited from Benjamin Hill himself. Who carries all this up here, but not back down? What kind of gluttony is this?

'You've got an entire restaurant up here, Johansen,' I say.

Johansen doesn't reply, instead he throws back his head slightly, making his hair tremble. His hair is dry, like wire wool. There's a bit of length at the back of his neck, but on top it's completely thinned out, and he has half-heartedly pushed the hair at the sides over his crown. It looks like some kind of Deleuzian comb-over frizz. When he shakes his head in a dramatic punctuation of one moment of the music or another, his hair sways firmly – a dry, hard swing, the way you can imagine tree moss swaying if the rock or trunk it's growing on is given a kick.

Almost imperceptibly, the notes coming from the piano become lighter and, as far as I can tell, less melancholic. Is Johansen obeying? Is he going for a major key? Or is this a modulation already in the piece? Old Johansen conjures the notes from the instrument with such ease. How is it possible for such fat, emperor-like fingers to move so freely and skilfully? How heavy is the piano? What a monster. What a beast. My chest tightens at the thought of the instrument once having to be hauled up here on to the mezzanine. It can't have come up the spiral staircase, that much is clear. But how then? There's a dormer window beneath the vault to the right, but it's no more than sixty centimetres wide, so it can't have been that way, either. Did they cut through the roof at some point, to haul this monstrous musical instrument inside? Did they haul old Johansen in at the same time?

'Is that Heifetz on the wall over there?' I ask, pointing –
even though Johansen is sitting with his back to it – to a
small, framed print squeezed in and half hidden behind
the stacks.

'It's Heifetz,' says Johansen.

'Funny, you can recognize him by the sharp nostrils.'

'It's not much to look at. The etching was done by a forgotten Norwegian printmaker. No Heifetz, exactly,' says
Johansen.

'No, no Heifetz.'

'Wonderful,' says Johansen, still without turning around.
The music is definitely lighter now. More lively.

'Great,' I say, ready to go back downstairs.

'Can I stop You for a moment?'

He actually uses the formal address on me. I turn back
and remember that I've been addressing Johansen infor-
mally for as long as I've been up here.

'Yeah?'

'I think You seem a bit frazzled.'

'What?'

'I think You seem hectic.'

'I'm not sure I understand.'

'Shaky. Frail.'

'Is that so?'

'It's like Winnicott claims,' Johansen says, accompanied
by his own now lively playing. 'The ego organizes defences
against the breakdown of the ego-organization.'

'And that is?'

'When the ego's organization falters, collapse rears its head, you know.'

So, I radiate wretchedness, even through my imaginary armour and shield of service, routine and predictability. Old Johansen doesn't even need to turn around to be able to sense my advanced wretchedness.

'I wonder that a soothsayer doesn't laugh whenever he sees another soothsayer,' Cicero said, or so I've heard, though probably he said it in Latin. And with that in mind, I think that the wretch's advantage is that he doesn't start crying when he sees another wretch, another poor beggar. I'm much more moved and affected by my own wretchedness than I am by other wretches who come into The Hills. I become easily annoyed by other wretches. There, I said it. And yet I allow my own wretchedness to preoccupy me. If I think about the causes of my own wretchedness – something I should avoid doing here – I can see that I have clear, understandable reasons for being a wretch. I might think that it's not my fault I've become wretched, might find it unfair that I have these shortcomings.

But if I see another wretch, I don't take into consideration the pitiful or unfair causes of his or her wretchedness. I just think that he or she should get a grip and not be so miserable. We all have our problems, I think, now make sure you pull yourself together. I stand, stooped, and think all this. Pull yourself together, I think in my stoopedness, about another person. At the sight of someone radiating one kind of misery or another, I think these things coldly and without compassion. I can stand there, completely crazed inside, stooped and crooked, over my own faults and failures, internal wounds which never heal. I can stand like that, utterly cold, and be irritated by a fellow wretched human and their faults, their cracks and their crookedness.

Scroll

Widow Knipschild has asked for crumble. I have placed it in front of her, followed by a dessert spoon which I put down, gentle as a cat's paw, above the cake plate. Grey, subdued and pale colours are the common thread, if I may say so, unifying Widow Knipschild's outfit. She is as colourless as ash. I've always liked her. Elegant lady. Intelligent being. She was a professor of cultural history in her day. 'You know,' she once said. 'You know I worked at the Plantin-Moretus Museum at the same time as I was studying in Antwerp?' I knew it, she had told me before, in her senile way. 'You know that back then, we actually sneaked in to print pamphlets on the old printing presses at night?' That I didn't know. 'I printed my first pamphlet on the oldest press there, which, as you might have heard, is the second-oldest preserved printing press in the world. And it's still in the same place where it has always been, since a handful of years after Gutenberg.

You can see it in the floor, its feet have eaten into the floor-boards.' 'Fantastic,' I said. 'Do you know what the first leaflet I printed said?' No, how could I have known that? 'It said, "The great are only great because we are on our knees. Let us rise up. Proudhon."' 'You don't say,' I said, surprised, following up with a question about whether she did the printing with the old lead type they have at the museum. 'Oh yes,' she said then. 'What else?' And then she cut off a piece of the pear tart I had placed in front of her, light as an eiderdown, and spent a long time savouring it before she finished off with: 'The reason I'm always here at The Hills is because it's the one place in Oslo – well, perhaps even the whole of Scandinavia – which reminds me most of the Plantin-Moretus.' 'That might be laying it on a bit thick,' I said. 'No, it isn't,' said Widow Knipschild.

I said before that I never use my phone during work hours, but that's gone a bit off the rails today. From time to time I have to check for news from Edgar, or possibly from Anna. It might be too early to expect a message, but what if they've sent one? I try to 'sneak' past the Chef, but in vain. The passage between his rounded back and the blackened, greasy, pan-covered wall on the way to the cramped wardrobe corner where my all-weather jacket is hanging is so narrow that it feels like a sexual act to squeeze through there. The Chef is frying mushrooms and onions, he's literally throwing the mushrooms and onions around in the frying pan. He tosses the mush-rooms and onions with firm flicks, so that they fly high in the air, almost a metre above the pan, or that's how it seems. He glares at the mushrooms and onions when they're at eye level. They hang in the air in front of his face. Then they fall, the slices of mushroom and slivers of onion, all together, back into the frying pan. Accompanying this tossing of vegetables are sharp elbow movements, his lower arm is moving back and forth like the piston of a locomotive, and I'm immediately concerned about passing behind him. What if I bump into him? I clear my throat. The Chef pauses. A sign that I can pass. The mushrooms and onions are sizzling, I'll have to hurry before they burn. He cooks at high temperatures, the Chef.

Anna has sent zero messages, and there's not a peep from Edgar either. It's only a little after ten. When will Anna arrive, I wonder. I use the two-hand, straight-arm phone technique typical of old people. The phone is in my left hand while a crooked finger pads across the screen like a dry croissant. I don't even understand how the phone can react to my jabbing fingertip. I watch some videos produced by drones while I'm in here, inside, out there, online. You have to deal with a lot of drone recordings nowadays. These drones have recorded crystal-clear images of a tank attack in the Jobar district of Damascus. Down in the toilets, here at the restaurant, there has long been a beautiful pattern of dark green and white stone on the floor, a pattern that reminds me of the old Damascus. Lovely stone. The drone images in my feed show a Damascus that looks, more than anything, like Widow Knipschild's crumble. Nothing but sand-coloured grains and lumps. The oldest continuously inhabited city in the world, that's what I'm seeing here, completely in ruins, before I hear a call from the kitchen.

I scroll a little more. That can't be illegal. Now I see an image of a girl standing on the hooves of a horse which is lying on its back, a bit like a dog. A cat that says 'cock'. A hand being chopped off, jihadi-style. An article about the relationship between screen radiation and the yellowing of teeth. What do you know. My teeth are fairly white. Maybe it's because of my limited screen time, in combination with my healthy scepticism of technology? An unexpected bonus. Why, and, not least, *how* would Anna have sent me a message at ten past ten? Using phones is bound to be forbidden at school – not that I know anything in particular about that. The agreement is clear. She'll come here when she's finished. Why would she bother texting? Does she even have a phone? And Edgar is probably on a plane or busy in his important meeting. The urgent business, as he called it. I send him a quick message:

THE MYSTERIES OF THE BRAIN AND THE HEART REVEAL THEMSELVES IN THE SMALL, REMARKABLE AND UNEXPECTED COMBIN-ATION OF LETTERS AND WORDS. YOU LEECH.

After that, I scroll a bit further. I see a puma looking after a tiny frog, a dwarf frog. A 105-year-old tells us that it might not be worth spending your entire life on a strict diet, free from processed meat, since the last thirty years are doomed to be repetitive and joyless anyway. I also see a girl wearing an Idi Amin uniform, a copy down to the very last detail, for Hallowe'en. She looks quite like him. A she-Amin in miniature.

'Hey,' I hear the Chef say from the kitchen. Is it me he's talking to as I stand here, besotted with my phone?

'Sorry?'

'They're calling for you.'

I shove my telephone back into my all-weather jacket before I expose myself in the most embarrassing way by having to squeeze past the Chef again. I strut into the restaurant with flared nostrils and scrolled-out eyes. The florist has cut the stamens from the lilies, OK, but what about the coloured kale from last week? Has he forgotten about that? The coloured kale, or ornamental kale, as the florist calls it, has started to smell. I catch a faint but undeniable hint of it, a sharp *note* in the air, tormenting us. Widow Knipschild sits in the middle of it, shrouded in her own cloud of perfume. But it's not her who needs my attention, nor is it the beer-drinking actor. It's the Maître D'.

'Tables 7 and 12 need serving,' he says firmly.

'Of course,' I say, looking at him without yielding, as I've learnt to do, despite my natural lack of authority – I've got a talent for this confrontational staring-back-at-someone. I might be completely in pieces on the inside, but to stand there with a waiter's idiotic, and equally impenetrable 'pride', staring back, well, that I can do. I don't give in. I use my face to say 'of course' back at the Maître D's face. The Maître D's face is shiny with lotion. He has a kind of wet look going on, combined with his dry hair. Isn't it supposed to be the other way around?

'And please, do something about that kale.'

'The florist was just here, should I get him back?'

'What do you need the florist for?'

'To sort out the kale.'

The Maître D' rubs his eyes. It looks completely grotesque. How can he put pressure on those bags without bursting them?

'What do you mean?' he says wearily.

'It's a poor show for the florist to leave the brassica from last week, smelling like death and manure,' I say. 'He should fix it.'

The Maître D' continues his rubbing, to my horror, while his left hand points dejectedly towards the bar. The romanesco is lying there.

'There's a lot of the stuff in here,' he says.

'Ah . . . of course,' I say, jolting towards the romanesco as though I had been given a prod behind the knees. 'The romanesco. I'm so sorry.'

'It was the young lady who drew my attention to it,' he says quietly, nodding his head quickly in the direction of Child Lady, who is still sitting over by the curtain.

'It?'

'That you had left the vegetable there.'

'Ah, you don't say,' I say, grabbing the romanesco with both hands, simultaneously feeling myself derail. 'What did she say?'

'She said that you left the cauliflower, the cabbage.'

'I understand.'

'It's good that you understand.'

'But what did she say?'

'What do you mean?'

'How did she say it?'

'How did she say it? By opening her mouth, I should think.'

'I see. But how could you know it was me she meant?'

The Maître D' stops his rubbing and lets his hand drop like a lead weight. He stands there for a few seconds with his eyes closed, as though he were sleeping upright, before slowly dragging them open again and bringing his surroundings back into focus, not unlike a mammal opening its eyes for the very first time.

'There was no misunderstanding,' he says, gaping.

'Of course not,' I say.

'. . .'

'But she can't have named me.'

' "Well, let's see!" said the blind man to the deaf man,' he says with satirical enthusiasm.

He doesn't need to do that to me.

The very tip of the romanesco is still pointing towards the bar stool where Child Lady was sitting before she moved. Vanessa hurries by with her dutiful stride, and I seize the opportunity to delegate.

'Hey,' I shout, a bit too harshly. Vanessa jumps. 'Can you call the florist?'

'Wasn't he just here?'

'Sadly, he didn't do his job properly.'

'I'll call him, then,' Vanessa says, scratching the stubble on her head.

Anna Arrives

Here comes Blaise Engelbert, vigorously, through the curtain. He has a *whiff* about him. He's really dressed up today. What a suit. We're all used to seeing quality suits in here, but this one is spectacular. The cut. The fabric. Sharper than inlaid Damascus steel. That might be a metaphor from the wrong cultural context, but it works all the same. If you can imagine translating British tailoring into traditional Syrian metalwork, well, then you can picture Blaise Engelbert right now – he's as sharp as damascened metal. I've never seen anything like it. Even the Maître D' gives him a quiet, but unmistakable, compliment, and that isn't something you see every day.

'I have to say,' I say as he passes.

'Yes,' Blaise says. He knows what I'm referring to.

'Yeah, that's really something,' I say abstractedly.

'Yup,' says Blaise.

I think you have to be my age to appreciate lapels like that. It's as though children – with all their hypersensitivity to food and that kind of thing – don't take in the important details. Children don't notice the small things. How a glowing light in the corner of a room can mean so infinitely much. How a good or bad chair can save or ruin an interior. And the opposite – how relaxed your sensory apparatus becomes by the time you're my age. I never get car sick, I can eat mouldy cheese and rotten fish. I can chomp on calluses and fibres without retching. I couldn't do that as a child. There can be as many lumps as you like in the soup. I can knock back schnapps without pulling a face. That's impossible for children. But if the door is ajar and I feel the slightest draught around my ankles, the faintest hint of cold, well, then I react. I react powerfully. Which door is open now, I wonder. As a child, I could wear wet shoes for hours without noticing. I would smell like a sheep when I came in again, my thick wool socks would be so wet. My nails were cracked, but I didn't realize until it was too late. I wouldn't have noticed Blaise Engelbert's masterful lapels as a nine-year-old. They would have been invisible to me. But now his lapels are all I can see. I've never seen anything like them.

Child Lady jumps up from the marble table, as though everything were choreographed, and follows Blaise over to table 10, my table. It's time for the pulling out of chairs. Child Lady gives Blaise her hand, Blaise takes it gallantly. I take hold of the back of the chair I assume Child

Lady will be sitting in, and pull it out while I 'indicate' with my other hand where she can/should/will/must sit down: here, on the chair I have pulled out.

'Thank you,' she says.

'Of course,' I say.

She moves so that the backs of her knees are in front of the seat and the fronts of her thighs are against the edge of the table, waiting for me to push in the chair. I catch a slight hint of musk again. It is musk, isn't it? She squats very slightly for a moment, with the great gluteus muscle – the gluteus maximus – fully tensed, waiting for me to push the chair beneath her, which I do, so that she can comfortably sit down.

'There,' she says.

I see thousands of possibilities for how I can parry this 'there', but I steer myself away from saying *voilà*, so, there now, excellent or anything else stupid. I control myself and breathe repeatedly through my nose, down into my moustache. Sensibly quiet, that's how I keep myself. Professionally and sensibly quiet.

Apropos controlling yourself, or the counterpoint of control, letting go; I must say that old Johansen took the change of mood seriously. The music on the mezzanine is presto now, so to speak. It's *vivace* on that raised, enlarged, ingrown bay of his, or is it called *vivo*? Is it *vif* the French call this kind of quick, cheery music, verging on the hectic? Is it a bit too lively? What does the Maître D' think about that? Don't we, the staff, in our jackets, black and white, take on a slightly comical character when accompanied by this *lebhafte* music? I wish he would tone down the mood a touch, Johansen.

There's something about that musky scent. It smells a bit like old lady, but on a young woman like Child Lady, it becomes rather special. Blaise also uses fragrance, and it's extremely subtle. His scent mixes with Child Lady's soft musk. What does Blaise use? There's a hint of Grey Vetiver there, but the wood note is different, the wood in his scent is closer to Encre Noire. More *Aquilaria*, or *oud*. You can detect a damper type of wood than in the Vetiver. Does he mix scents? Very few men do. Is Blaise so advanced? He probably is. I almost feel high on these scents now. A cheerful mix of smells, like Anna talked about. That's the kind of progress we want here at The Hills. She should have been here now. In here, we want unexpected combinations and mixes of the highest, best qualities. We want, figuratively speaking, eggs to be plucked from hens, and for the paste of crushed and ground sunflower seeds to be pressed until the oil runs out, and for this oil to be mixed with the egg and whipped hard, so that the whole thing changes character and becomes mayonnaise. That's what we want, like I said, figuratively speaking. Blaise's and Child Lady's scents have an almost magical effect when mixed, equivalent to the miracle of mayonnaise. Something completely new and special occurs between them, between their aromas, their bouquets. (How to describe mayonnaise to someone who has only ever tasted sunflower seeds and eggs on their own?)

Through the window, I notice that The Pig is being

driven to the door, in a car that can't be described as anything but a *ride*. It's exactly one thirty, his usual time. I show The Pig to the table where Blaise is already glittering in his suit, Child Lady glowing by his side.

'Are we expecting anyone else?' I ask, bobbing up and down on my toes.

'Just the three of us,' says The Pig.

'Three it is.' I begin to clear away the fourth setting. 'Can I tempt you with anything before your food?'

'I'll risk a glass of the white burgundy.'

'Wonderful.'

I place the white burgundy in front of The Pig's hand, light as a soap bubble. He nods in thanks and touches the crystal, runs his index finger and stumpy thumb up and down the stem. Then he solemnly lifts the glass and sips. Child Lady glances upwards, as though she is twelve years old and I am a friend of her father's and she is The Pig's daughter and The Pig is my friend. Her smile is delivered with a closed mouth at first, but then she parts her lips. It's like a curtain being raised from her much-discussed dental arch. Child Lady gives me the whole row of pearly whites, her smile crushes everything else around it.

* * *

It's approaching quarter to two. The time of day when children Anna's age finish school, I think. Or is it? Does she go to any clubs? After-school activities? If Edgar had given me a time, I would have been able to avoid falling into speculation about Anna's arrival. I quickly squeeze past the Chef and into the wardrobe corner. Zero messages. Once again, I'm staring at a blank screen, but a bit of scrolling can't be prohibited. First, I see a picture of SpongeBob balancing two corn on the cobs, one on each eyeball, then a '90s recording of Eminem rapping about pickles as he fries onion rings in Detroit. I also learn that Jewish families who fled from the Nazis are now seeking German passports because of conditions in the UK. Damn Edgar.

* * *

Vanessa, with her close-cropped hair, traipses over with the florist. He's behind her, in his florist's uniform, which is essentially a gardener's outfit; working clothes. Robust trousers with a set of functional pockets. A pair of gloves sticking out of one. Now I have to grill him a little. We don't want any stench in here.

'Hey!' I say, with my characteristic lack of timing. 'Florist!' I blurt out. The florist reacts. As does the Maître D', who is standing over by table 17. He looks at me like a deep-sea angler-fish, with bulging eyes and an unhappy mouth, the wall lamp sticking out from a panel just to the left of his face like one of those antennae with a glowing lump that those fish have. 'One moment,' I say, holding my fingers in the air while I move my left hand, with the bandage, behind my back. The florist leans against the bar and studies my walk over to him. My footsteps clomp against

the pretty mosaic floor. He can watch my head movements, the hen-like motion, the strutting. The stoop. I
wonder whether I'll manage to keep up the momentum.

'Hey,' I say.

'Yes?'

'The colourful kale.'

'The decorative kale, yes.'

'Do you notice it?'

'Do I notice it?'

I flare my nostrils and 'sniff' gently with my big nose,
then give a brief 'wave' with one hand to signify 'odour'.

'Do you notice the kale?' I repeat.

'Can't you just tell me what you want?'

'It stinks.'

'Then you need to take it out,' says the florist.

'Well, you can carry it out, then.'

'I was up at Høybråten,' says the florist. 'Did you make
me drive all the way back here just to carry a withered
plant outside?'

I take hold of his upper arm, not too hard, but firmly,
and lead him towards Blaise and Child Lady. We stop two
metres from their table. I draw in more air through my
nostrils to signal that he should do the same.

'Smell,' I say. The florist sniffs cautiously. I tell him that
this is the scent scape we aim for at The Hills. *Oud. Aquilaria*. Mixed with gastronomic aromas.

'The scent scape?' The florist looks confused. Now I
pull him over to the bar, where there is a huge arrangement of musty decorative kale.

'Not this,' I say.

'Are you serious?'

'Yes, you bet your life I am.' I ask him to inhale.

'Honestly,' says the florist.

'Your work, or lack of it,' I continue, 'has disturbed the scent scape. You need to ensure smooth blooming.'

The florist tries to explain that plants don't have an expiry date. 'If something withers between Monday and Friday, surely you can just throw it out?'

'As I said,' I say, and like a police officer, I grip his arm, but with the wrong hand – the bandage twists and the blister stings. I try to swap hands, but in my fumbling the florist snatches his arm away.

'Don't touch me,' he says. He pulls back and shakes his head irritably. I try to grab him again, but just end up shoving his shoulder with an awkward right hand.

'Stop it,' he says, moving with tetchy, floristic steps towards the exit. I'm knocked off kilter, off balance, tilted. Then he disappears behind the curtain. The florist is not happy now. I wonder whether he'll ever be back to do his floristry, or de-floristry, if you can put it like that, here at The Hills.

And, as if that wasn't enough: as I'm standing there, staring after the raging florist, two small hands appear and part the curtains by the entrance. Anna (nine) peers in. Here she is. My insides flip. She bends down. A good distance above her head, an outstretched shirtsleeve appears. The curtain moves to one side. Who does this bony hand belong to? My gut churns. Anna takes a step forward, and in comes Sellers, tall as he is. Bewitching as he is. The scamp is standing in the doorway. On his face, he is wearing the biggest smile of all, as is fitting for a scamp.

'Sweet girl,' he says to me with a wink.

PART V

Holbein

'They say that Hans Holbein the Younger's portrait sketch of Baron Wentworth is damaged and doesn't bear Holbein's distinctive left-handed hatching,' Blaise says eagerly. 'They say that the drawing may have been tampered with at a later date. The hat and the ear are flat as a pancake, fair enough, and the head of hair is perhaps a little uninspired. The dirty ink spot giving the right eye definition against the brim of the hat is undoubtedly a later addition. But everyone who has had this drawing in front of them' – and now Blaise puts his shoulder to the wheel to carry his audience (Sellers) with him, and spells it out with emphasis – 'everyone who has seen this drawing one-on-one, live, with their own eyes, knows that it's first-rate.'

Blaise says all this to Sellers, shamelessly, standing by Sellers' table, table 13, gesticulating, with The Pig by his side. He is speaking loudly enough for me to hear everything as I hide here, behind the pillar, waiting for a sign. They'll probably seal the deal with something to eat or drink soon. That's how adults behave.

'The facial hair beneath Wentworth's nose,' Blaise continues, 'is comparable in terms of genius to the way Sir Thomas Wyatt's moustache is depicted, no more, no less. The contouring on the bridge of his nose is formidable. *Exceptional.* That bridge is second to none. Literally. It's on a par with the highlights of Velázquez's Pope Innocent X's lower lip. I mean it. Big words, but that's the way it is. The colouring on Wentworth's nose and nostrils, which is impossible to capture in reproductions, is so subtle, so delicate and über-minimal that there's no equal. Taken as a whole, including the clumsiness of the hat, the feather and the shadow from the brim, the drawing is a mystery. As with many of Holbein's Tudor drawings, it's difficult to say when, and by whom, the ink contours were added, if not by Holbein himself. Were they applied in order to transfer the image to a woodblock or canvas? The silver point, when was that added? The brushwork ranges from masterful to simple. None of Holbein's drawings contains more contradictions than the sketch of Wentworth, and they raise one another to the highest of artistic heights. At the same time, the drawing is vanishingly faint. Almost invisible.'

'And what's the point here?' Sellers wants to know.

'Well, it's that I want you to come and take a look at the drawing,' says Blaise, still wearing his spectacular suit jacket. 'I have it at home.'

'That can't be true,' says Sellers.

'Yes, come with me and you'll see.'

'No, lay off it,' says Sellers.

But Blaise smiles triumphantly and nods slowly. 'You know, Holbein's Tudor drawings aren't out in frames in the library at Windsor. They're in an acid-free box. In a pile. Some have a mount, others don't. But we can't talk about that out here. We can smooth over the details at my place,' he says, quietly.

'No, that's a bit much,' says Sellers. 'That needs digesting. We need a bit of cheese for that.' He shouts: 'Roll out the cheese!'

Blaise nods and waves intently in my direction. Time for the trolley! With a bit of cheese, they'll celebrate that contact has been established. We have a three-tier cheese trolley. The tiers present a selection of cheeses, and on top there are two copper pots containing, respectively, walnuts in a red-wine reduction and a winter-fruit compote.

To recap Anna's and Sellers' entrance once more: Sellers held the curtain for Anna and allowed her to slip in ahead of him. Smiling, he walked behind her to his usual table. He gave me a quick hello, like he usually does, as I stood there welcoming him, before the shock came: Sellers shouted a 'Hey there!' as he passed Child Lady's table, where The Pig and Blaise were also sitting. Child Lady said hello back, and the two men nodded politely.

And with that, the connection between tables 10 and 13 has been established, I thought to myself. Everything is going just as The Pig planned. He's pleasant and sociable, The Pig, but he's sly, I've always said that. So sly. He has deliberately used Child Lady to get to Sellers. He used me at first, trying to get hold of me to talk about this and that, then he turned to Child Lady. She is the perfect collaborator.

After that, no more than five or six minutes passed before Child Lady sat down at table 13, in Sellers' seat of honour. Conversation flowed. She touched Sellers on the forearm as she laughed. There was some gesturing towards The Pig's table. The Pig and Blaise were like two glowing light bulbs. Then she was spinning an invisible thread between the two tables, two otherwise separate worlds, tables 10 and 13. Child Lady gestured for The Pig and Blaise to come over. And, just like that, Blaise and The Pig were standing by table 13 in their fancy suits, talking about the Holbein until Sellers couldn't believe his ears.

'It can't be true,' Sellers said. 'What a joke.'

It was discussed back and forth for a good fifteen minutes after that. And then they wanted cheese. And as I now push the cheese trolley over to table 13, Blaise and The Pig have cause to sit down. As I stand behind the cheese trolley, slicing a piece of Comté for Blaise, a piece of Port Salut for Sellers, and so on, while they discuss whether it's a real or a fake Holbein that Blaise is meant to have at his place, and as Child Lady sits there casting glances across the otherwise hobo-like table, I find the experience humiliating. I don't know why, but I really do.

'A bit of the Reblochon, too,' Blaise says mid-chomp. 'I really like cow's milk cheese. Don't you prefer cow?'

'Yes, so long as it's smear-ripened,' says The Pig.

'Port Salut is smear-ripened, God help me,' says Sellers. 'And I should think it's cow?' He glances at me, equal measures of questioning, mocking and drunkenness in his eyes.

'The Port Salut is made from cow's milk,' I confirm.

'I'll take a bit of chèvre,' Child Lady says with a chuckle. She is a complete and utter consumer. And that's how the first hour passes.

In that hour, Anna has been doing her homework, with hairclips at her temples and a plait down her back, her rucksack by the side of the classic marble-top. Who plaits her hair in the morning? I jumped when she came in, even though I had been waiting for her all day. Yes, I really jumped.

'Go over to your table, Anna,' I said, a bit too loudly, going out into the kitchen and hurrying back with four kinds of sausage arranged on a plate, which I placed in front of her as light as an autumn leaf. 'You can enjoy this sausage before dinner.'

'Thanks.'

'Would you like anything to drink?'

'Just water.'

'No apple juice? We have the good one from Abildsø.'

'No, thanks. It's a bit floury.'

'Oh? I think it's both delicate and tasty.'

'I think I'll have water.'

'Then water you shall have.'

Anna pulled out her school books. I poured water.

At table 13, they're wolfing down their cheese. They've quaffed the dessert wine I thoughtfully recommended. The mood now is worryingly jovial. Sellers really is in the mood. He's doling out his pickpocket-like charm. And, as expected, he'll want a nip of something stronger. He raises his arm and waves. The others at the table are on board. They want a snifter too. It's half past five, but that won't stop them. The Pig, Blaise and Child Lady nod when Sellers suggests they should all have one.

'Anna,' I say on my way over to the bar, to the alcohol.

'Yes?'

'I've got something to show you.'

'Oh.'

'Have you finished your homework?'

'Almost, I just have maths to do.'

'What kind of maths is it?'

'Division with decimal numbers.'

'I've almost forgotten how to do that.'

'It's OK.'

'Is it without a calculator?'

'Everyone can do division with a calculator.'

(. . .)

'Give me a wave when you've finished, and I'll show you something.'

'OK.'

'Oh, also?'

'Yes?'

'Do you have a phone?'

'No.'

'Do you know when your dad is coming?'

'No, but I guess he'll just come here,' says Anna.

'Yes, I suppose he will.'

I signal 'four snifters' to the Bar Manager and slope off towards the kitchen. Where's the romanesco? Has the Chef seen the romanesco? Yes, he uses his knife to point to the counter, where it's lying with the quince and something else green. I grab the vegetable with both hands and notice as I do that the bandage around my blister is slack and disgusting. I'll have to change it. With an 'Excuse me', I squeeze past the Chef and into the wardrobe corner. Nothing from Edgar. I send him a message.

ANNA IS DOING HER HOMEWORK. BEEN HERE
A GOOD HOUR. HOW ARE YOU GETTING ON?

The logic, Edgar often says, is that life in the big city is so sad that we may as well sell it for money. But no one profits from his lack of punctuality. I leave the bandage as it is and squeeze back past the Chef to serve the drinks to table 13. Sellers knocks his back practically before I've even put it down. The others follow suit. They immediately order another round. One snifter rarely remains just the one.

Anna waves to me. She has finished her maths.

'Did you manage it?' I say.

'Yes, of course.'

'I want to show you something fun.'

With a finger in front of my face, meant to illustrate 'look', I bring out the romanesco from behind my back and gently place it on the marble table top in front of her. She looks at it, then at me. I explain that it's a romanesco cauliflower.

'Isn't it very special?'

'Yes,' Anna agrees. I laugh warmly, but my laugh is like the brief honk of an air horn, more aggressive than disarming.

'You can draw this to pass the time.' Anna nods. Then I launch into my speech about fractals and Mandelbrot, just like I did with Child Lady. Anna listens. She asks who M. C. Escher is.

'Well, let me tell you,' I say, continuing to teach. 'And that's not all. It tastes great. And it's healthy. If you like, I can ask the Chef to steam it for you, so you can have it for dinner. Draw first and eat later,' I say, followed by another quick honk of the 'laughter horn'. Anna nods and nods.

Wax Crayon

The Bar Manager wants to talk. She's reacting to the gathering at table 13.

'What kind of event is this?' she wants to know.

'It's something about them wanting Sellers to go home with them to look at a drawing,' I explain.

'That seems unlikely. Why? A valuation? In that case, it's Raymond they should be asking. Sellers has no idea.'

'But Raymond always comes with that charlatan Bratland in tow,' I point out, 'and no one wants *him* around. And with such an elegant girl as her, the young one, at the table, it's impossible to spend time with Bratland. He's always looking for a leg-over, he's a perv. He's a phony.'

The Bar Manager's reasoning is that The Pig and Blaise have seized their chance now that Bratland isn't hanging around Sellers, for once.

I set a few tables. Tablecloths and underlays are smoothed down. The crumber comes out. My eyes restlessly sweep the room. I take in everything. I really do. I know how far Anna has got in her drawing of the romanesco. I know which drinks have and haven't been drunk at table 13. Child Lady seems restless. But she has nowhere to go now, does she? Everyone of interest is already sitting at table 13. What's next? My eyes are locked in a duel with the Maître D's; his eyes see everything mine see, and possibly even more. I mistakenly serve a roulade to a group of diners at table 8. He points to the roulade and I carry it away before the diners manage to remark on my mistake.

'What should we make of this?' the Maître D' asks.

'I'm sorry,' I say.

'If you're born a penny, you'll never be a dollar,' he says.

I can feel my right eye getting bloodshot.

Before I know it, Child Lady is standing next to Anna, bent over her drawing. Damn her, she's quick as a flash. Does Anna have to be dragged into this mess too? Without blinking, I hurry over to them.

'What's going on here?' I say, but my question just bounces off them. I don't have the authority to cut through their talk. Child Lady doesn't even look up.

'When I was little,' she says to Anna, 'I always had such a crazy number of projects on the go. I was completely in my own little world. I could sit for hours cutting pictures out of magazines.' Isn't that typical. Child Lady talks with emotion about her childhood, to hint that she hasn't moved past it and has remained fundamentally naive.

Now she puts her nail to the drawing, to a spot where Anna has missed something.

'I used to wash all the time,' she says to Anna. 'I declared war on germs. I refused to hurry in the mornings.' She giggles. 'I declared war on time. I declared war on worry. I declared war on darkness. I declared war on quiet. I declared war on fat.' Anna continues to draw. 'And then I declared war on war,' Child Lady says, looking at me.

'So I'm not the only one to be served this handsome cauliflower?' she adds.

'Yes, Anna was going to try to draw it.'

'I don't know if I can get any more of the detail,' Anna says.

'It's a very nice drawing. I'll leave you two alone,' says Child Lady.

Anna waves to her.

'How sweet!' Child Lady says, waving back. 'She's flirting with me. Are you flirting with me, Anna?'

This is verging on reckless. Anna isn't flirting. Children don't 'flirt', the way mothers and women always claim that they do. It's Child Lady doing the flirting. She flirts and seduces, even when she isn't trying to seduce anyone. There's something strange about Child Lady. From a certain distance, she looks like an angel, but close up, like a devil. She goes back to Sellers' table and sits down by Blaise. Damn it, how to get rid of her?

'You've really captured the pattern, Anna,' I say.

'But it's completely impossible!'

'You've even drawn the lines showing how the endless

pattern in the conical shape follows spiral formations inwards and inwards. I think it's fantastic, Anna.'

Child Lady forces herself back into the conversation at table 13. I don't know what I should say about her appearance over there. It seems like the 'simplest' things are the most painful for Child Lady. The most 'human' are the most mechanical. She is optimistic, positive, satisfied, enthusiastic, cheerful. In other words: she's suffering.

'Who was that lady?' Anna asks.

'Oh, she's Mr Graham's friend. The dapper old man who's always at table 10.'

'She smelled nice.'

'Everything concrete in this world has disappeared up between Child Lady's bum cheeks, I've thought to myself,' I say.

Anna shrieks with laughter. 'Child Lady?'

'Yes. Two minutes, and your dinner will be ready.'

It's a bizarre scene that's playing out at Sellers' table. They're discussing the Holbein sketch, and Sellers seems very interested. But then, in some strange way, he manages to get the wrong end of the stick by asking detailed questions about how the wax crayon has been applied to the paper. Blaise explains that Holbein didn't use *crayons*, of course. But Sellers keeps talking about it.

'Crayons are handy,' he says, 'they're good for making marks underwater. I've often bought crayons from Karmøy Diving Services. They've got a good selection and such reasonably priced packs of twelve.'

'The drawing has the faintest chalk colouring. That would be impossible to achieve with crayons,' Blaise corrects him. 'I don't even know if they had crayons back then. Possibly oil pastels?'

'I'm not talking about oil pastels, Blaise,' says Sellers. 'Who in their right mind would say "Holbein" and "oil pastel" in the same sentence? What kind of nonsense is this? You can get wax crayons at Hansmark, too.'

'Hansmark?' asks Blaise.

'Yes, at Hansmark they stock the Lyra brand of pencil. They'll write on any surface. Even dusty, rusty, oily or wet. They also have a sharpener built into the lid.'

'I don't think we're on the same page right now,' says Blaise.

'It sounds like you're talking about a workman's pencil,' says The Pig.

'Should we have another round of drinks?' says Sellers.

'Yes, can do,' says The Pig. He turns to Child Lady. 'Are you drinking?'

'Shouldn't I be?' she says.

'Of course!'

'Then let's all drink,' says Blaise.

'Yes, let's,' says Sellers. 'Another round over here!'

'Another round of drinks,' I say.

'We want more,' says Blaise. He's cheery.

'Snifters all round,' says Sellers.

Child Lady looks up.

'Could I have an Amaretto?' she says.

'Definitely,' I say.

'Ah, liqueurs made from pistachio nuts are never wrong!' says Sellers. 'Good choice.'

'Pistachio?' says Blaise.

'Amaretto, the liqueur of nuts,' says Sellers.

The poise Child Lady displays as she sits between Sellers and Blaise is more like an accountant's than a dancer's. I stride behind the bar, hunchbacked, and relay the Amaretto order.

'Did he say pistachio?' asks the Bar Manager.

'He did,' I say.

I carry over Anna's lasagne with pecorino, the way she likes it, with a green salad on the side, plus a Coke, and the steamed romanesco on its own plate. I say that the romanesco is mostly for fun's sake. She doesn't have to eat the whole thing. No, she says, she wants to. Then she catches sight of the bandage.

'Have you hurt your hand?'

'Yes, I managed to give myself a horrible blister in the cellar.'

'The bandage is dirty. Haven't you changed it?'

'No, it happened yesterday.'

'I can help you after I've eaten,' she says. 'I've done first aid at school.'

The cheese topping on the lasagne is scalding hot, Anna knows that, which is possibly why she tackles the romanesco first. Or is she actually curious? It's nice that she shows interest in my ideas. She holds the fork like a stick and cuts off a bit of the cauliflower.

'It tastes nice,' she confirms with a quick nod.

'Would you like some pepper on your pasta?'

'Yes, please.'

I fetch the biggest peppermill to grind over it, the one she's always liked. The Maître D' catches me on my way back.

'We'll have to try not to make it as late today,' he says.

'Sorry?'

'With the child.'

'No, of course,' I say.

'Only a scoundrel gives away more than he owns, you know.'

Edgar says that one of the most important qualities for modern man, if that's an actual concept, is mastering excess. What if you don't have this quality? Then you're in a pickle. I'm not always so good at filtering or sorting the continual stream of things, this pressure. And the Maître D' really doesn't help by sending these barbs in my direction, making my defences crack. Can't I give the girl a sprinkling of pepper without him bothering me? I return to Anna and season her lasagne with three firm twists.

The Gauze Bandage

And they're at it again, at table 13. Sellers asks me to come closer. I half kneel to hear what he's saying. In surfing, there's something called a tuck knee. You push your knee sideways to achieve a lower centre of gravity. The concept also works in skateboarding and snowboarding. I have tuck knee now. I hold the bandaged hand behind my back. Let me put it like this: having tuck knee here at The Hills is different from riding a swell in the Pacific or along a concrete storm drain in Santa Monica. Here at The Hills, tuck knee means awkwardness, not style. Subordination. Obedience. Weakness.

'It might seem a little unorthodox, but could we order some food now?' he says.

'But you've already had cheese?' I say.

'Then we'll have to think outside the box.' He laughs with a deep, whistling smoker's cough.

Everything is on its head now. All is out of place. It's

like a state of emergency in here. They had the cheese first. Then the digestifs. After the digestifs, they want dinner. I hesitate. Sellers looks at me.

'We can manage it,' he says.

'I'm sure you can,' I say, 'but can I just see to one quick thing before I take your orders? There's just one thing.'

'Of course. Do your thing.'

I hurry over to Anna. She has just begun her lasagne.

'Anna, can I interrupt you a minute?' Anna smiles. 'Do you want to change the bandage on the blister now?'

'Sure,' she says, with her characteristic lack of hesitation. She gets up. 'Where?' she says.

'We'll have to go to the cellar to fetch more gauze bandage,' I explain. 'Do you want to come? It's a very special cellar.' She does. With enthusiastic steps she walks ahead of me through the curtains, out of the door, round the building and over to the cellar hatch. It's as cold as always. It's been dark for some time now, and the neon sign on the other side of the street makes my hands look alternatingly a washed-out salmon pink or a pale green. Anna seems excited as I fumble with the lock and key. I smile apologetically. Her face changes colour.

I stand with my left foot on the bottom step and tell Anna to come down.

'The stairs are really steep. You have to turn around and go backwards,' I explain. Anna turns around and moves slowly, with her heels first. Her feet are well wrapped up in a pair of oversized Moon Boots.

'Moon Boots, Anna?' I say.

'Yes,' she says. My hand is ready, the healthy one, in case she falls, but I don't touch her. She finishes crawling down and peers around the cellar.

'Wow,' she says. It's clear she has never seen anything like it. 'Look at the wine barrels. Are they real? How far back does it go?' Anna says.

'Far. I'm not sure.'

It's not light enough for us to make it to the drawer section that contains jute, gauze bandages, rags, towels, slings, spools, patches, doilies, aprons, decorative covers and cloths. I'll have to find the switch for the light bulb in the next section of corridor. Anna asks where the gauze bandage is. I think it's straight ahead and then round the corner to the right, the opposite way to the fruit, vegetables and romanesco.

'Two seconds, and I'll switch on the other light.' I fumble along the wall and twist a knob, but then the light goes on behind the steps. 'That wasn't right,' I say with a smile. But Anna is gone. This is perilous. I can't see her. I'm standing with the back of my head against the cellar roof. Everything but the so-called poker face falls away. In the mirror in the mornings, I see the violent decay ravaging what was once me. I imagine that same decay is also going on inside, in my brain, in my liver, in the erectile tissue of my penis. And definitely in my nervous system. The purely physical decay of the nerves can partly explain the relationship between youthful confidence and the fact that you become crushed by doubt as you grow older.

Shouldn't it be the other way around? Shouldn't you become more self-confident as the years pass? I try to think positively. I see my tired, weary face in the mirror every day, and say to myself: this is the youngest you'll look for the rest of your life.

'Are the bandages on this side or the far side?' Anna shouts.

I hear a giggle.

'The far side,' I say loudly.

It goes quiet. Then I hear a scraping sound. Then another long moment of silence.

A loud thud accompanied by a metallic clang makes me jump.

'Whoops!' I hear Anna say. 'Sorry!'

'Should I come over?' I say.

'Just stay there.'

There's a pretend cough. Some mumbling, followed by a gasp. More whispering. Then silence.

'Hello?' I say.

Another gasp. She's not crying? Now it's quiet again. Then I hear the padding of feet. Here she comes. The floor is covered in earth. Anna is carrying the gauze bandage in both hands. It's a big roll, the size of a Christmas brawn. Her smile is splendid. Perhaps it would be best to keep her down here, where things stand still. I could close the hatch. Lock her up. Lock Child Lady out.

'Come on, Anna,' I say, shooing her up the stairs.

Orders Reversed

I lead Anna into the men's toilet with the old-Damascus floor, so she can help me. I sit down on the toilet lid and unwind the old bandage. The blister and the flap of skin are disgusting. Blood, pus and dirt have soaked into the material. Anna kneels down in front of me and studies the flap. Concentrating, she starts to apply the new bandage. She turns the big roll of bandage 180 degrees with each layer, so that it spreads out in an impressive adder-like pattern from my palm. She moves her tongue from one corner of her mouth to the other in concentration.

'Do you have a safety pin or a bandage hook?' Anna says.

Her face is smooth, but slightly purple under the eyes. A clear sign of sleep deprivation. Edgar's wantonness is affecting the girl.

'The bandage isn't the self-adhesive sort, it's old,' she says.

'I just tied it yesterday,' I say.

She takes one of the clips from her hair and fastens the end by my wrist. I'm very impressed by her ingenuity.

'You really know your stuff.'

'Yessir,' says Anna.

'You must feel like having the rest of your lasagne now.'

Sellers is smirking. Child Lady slowly drifts in his direction. I can think only of abstract ways to describe her. She's the path we walk down to lose ourselves, I think now. She's not acting, she doesn't put on airs. It's as though her image puts on *her*.

The bandage is nice and tight. I feel a bit more energetic.

'Are we ready to order, then?' I say as I run my good hand between the guests and give the tablecloth a good de-crumbing.

Sellers says that they might 'go' with the main course now, they can look at the starters later. Child Lady asks if the Chef can prepare her some mushrooms again. Chanterelles, ideally, and she'd like to have some forest lambs too, if there are any.

'Actually, I think there are,' I say.

'Both rapeseed oil and butter,' she says. 'A few shallots. That's all. Well done. Iron pan. The mushrooms can't be allowed to boil.'

'That's routine in the kitchen,' I say. Blaise applauds her order. Then he smacks his tongue gently, as though he still has Reblochon stuck on the roof of his mouth and wants to see which main will best follow the cheese, an absurdity in itself. He decides on an Italian veal steak from the menu of the day which I, reliably, have chalked up on the board. Blaise pronounces *vitello alla sarda* with impressive intonation, and wants it served traditionally but also with potatoes – 'and peas, actually' – to the side of the spinach, the chanterelles and the sauce.

With a refined hand gesture, The Pig indicates that it's Sellers' turn, but Sellers says that The Pig can order first.

'No, after you,' says The Pig.

'No, you first,' Sellers insists. But when The Pig says 'grouse', Sellers quickly says 'plaice' over the top of him, making their words blend together.

'Pardon?' I say.

The Pig tries a new 'grouse', but Sellers' timing is perfect, this time he says 'kid' on top of The Pig's order, mixing everything up.

'Sorry, you go first.' The Pig smiles.

'No, you first, of course,' Sellers says, gesturing his concession.

The Pig peers through his varifocals and down at the menu, pretends to be reading it once more. 'Could I have . . .'

He runs a dry finger beneath the grouse dish. Blaise nods approvingly at Child Lady.

'Hmmm . . .' says The Pig.

He draws it out, peers at Sellers over the rim of his spectacles, then he gets ready. 'G . . .' he says.

'T . . .' says Sellers, like a flash of lightning.

The Pig tries a feint.

'Gr . . .'

'Ta . . .' Sellers quickly says.

(. . .)

'Grouse for Mr Graham, tartare for Mr Sellers,' I say, not siding with either of them.

'Could I have the Worcestershire sauce in an egg cup on the side?' says Sellers.

'Of course.'

'And do the chives come from the Chef's mother's garden?'

'I believe so,' I confirm.

'Could you ask him *not* to use those?'

'Absolutely,' I say.

'The soil in the Chef's mother's garden is affected by her living right next to the racetrack,' Sellers says quietly to the table. 'The chives taste stale.'

Sellers wants a beer with his tartare, but he butts in and corrects Blaise's French as Blaise orders a burgundy.

'There's more emphasis on the *u*,' he says. 'Burgúndy.'

'OK, so you mean Bourgogne?' Blaise says.

'Indeed, more [buʁ.]-gogne,' says Sellers.

'Yes, I agree with that,' says Blaise. 'If you have the [gɔɲ] at the end there. So [buʁ.gɔɲ].'

'Yes, but you can't be sloppy with the *ú*. We're practically talking [ʊ̈].'

'That's where I fall short.'

Amlost Over

I manage to make the Chef's copper pans rattle horribly when I go to check for messages from Edgar. The screen is still blank. My head feels tight. Anna can't sit here for ever, and she's getting tired. Maybe a bit of scrolling will help dampen the unease? A bird gets its beak caught in an emo's piercing. The urban myth that Abraham Lincoln, John F. Kennedy and Martin Luther King Jr. were all shot at ten past ten is false, I read here. Lincoln was shot at quarter past, and didn't die until early the next morning. Kennedy was killed at half past twelve, in the very middle of the day. King was shot at one minute past six in the evening, and pronounced dead at five past seven. The fact that watches in adverts are always set to ten past ten is purely aesthetic, not mythical, I learn. Shockingly, the next thing to appear is a picture of Edgar. He is smiling next to someone in a dark suit, along with an older gentle-man with an exceptionally bald head. To one side is a woman who looks like Michelle Obama would have looked if she was a Slav, Slavic. Someone uploaded the picture half an hour ago. Doesn't that look like Copenhagen in the background? It's not Oslo, at any rate.

YOU AREN'T STILL IN COPENHAGEN?

The spire in the background might be Sankt Andreas Kirke. I can't restrain myself from leaving a comment beneath the picture, anonymously. *The kids' programmes are amlost over*, I write. I notice the spelling mistake too late. Amlost. That's out there for anyone to read now. I'm the internet's most useless troll. It's well past seven, so it's going to fill up in here within the hour. There are limits to how much attention I can give Anna over the evening. Edgar needs to reply. I post a new message, anonymously. *I see you online in Copenhagen*, I write. Another misjudgement. Online and Copenhagen are, strictly speaking, two different places.

Anna is sitting at her table, she's reading sweetly, now with four clips in her hair, not five. I look at her with scrolled-out eyes. The colourful book cover suggests another fantasy novel. She has almost eaten all her romanesco. I explain that Edgar isn't replying right now, so there'll probably be a bit more of a wait. She doesn't seem to mind.

'Are you tired?' I ask.

'Not really.' But her eyes tell a different story. I offer to get her some of the Chef's twine so she can finger-weave a potholder or something. She says she's fine reading.

The Maître D' is hunched over the reservations book.

'The table where the girl is sitting is reserved from seven thirty,' he says. 'How long is she going to be here?'

'I don't know, unfortunately.'

'Are you responsible for her?'

'I suppose I am.'

'When poverty comes in at the door, love jumps out of the window,' he says and turns away.

'What do you mean by that?'

'After seven thirty, you'll have to find somewhere else for her.'

I head off to the bar to fetch the drinks for Sellers' table. While the Bar Manager pours the burgundy, she tells me that Blaise and The Pig are pestering Sellers now. And Child Lady is contributing, saying it's not far to Blaise's place and offering to be his 'wing-girl', apparently.

'Wing-girl? What kind of word is that?'

'I don't know. They're insisting on Sellers following Blaise home.' I zone out. My windpipe is tight now. 'Sellers is difficult,' she says. 'He's incredibly gentle and accommodating, but it's also impossible to get him to crack.' The Bar Manager is fired up. I am cursing Edgar. Cursing Blaise. Child Lady. Damn you all to hell.

Nest

This is really dragging on. Thanks to Edgar, I have no idea when my shift will end. He's keeping me trapped here. I'm tired. He's also forcing me past the Chef, into the wardrobe area, to the phone in my all-weather-jacket pocket, meaning I'm repeatedly having small doses of the loathsome present-day forced upon me. Nowness makes me unwell.

YOU REALLY NEED TO GET IN TOUCH NOW.

Edgar has (ironically) sat here himself, complaining about this intrusion, this stream of impressions. 'It's been said before,' he's said to me, 'and it'll probably be said again, but right now, today, I feel that under these conditions, it's enough. The transfer of information we're exposed to has never been more aggressive than it is today. No, there have never been more of these transmissions than there are today, and you can say the same of every day that passes. The necessary processing of impressions is no longer a possibility for me,' Edgar has said. 'Today it's over the top. I can't swallow these streams any more. It all became too much today. It's like wanting a glass of water and being given a bucketful to the face. The stream has never been stronger. Today, the stream was too strong. Never have I been more stuffed than today, on this last day in the series of all days. The feed has never been shriller. It's completely crazy now. So shrill. So violent.' These are Edgar's words. And now he himself is hovering out there, so to speak, online in Copenhagen, floating into the phone in my coat pocket, and dragging me out there, but not even answering. It's just under half an hour until Anna has to leave the table.

I hear Sellers arguing that it's Raymond who is the art expert, that they can call Raymond for him to come round and give them a valuation. 'Raymond?' the others ask.

'Yes, that whale who's often with me,' says Sellers. 'The guy with the typically south-Scandinavian look. An enormous, classic south Scandinavian.' Yes, they remember him. But they're not sure, since he's always with that third man, who is so brash.

'Bratland?' Sellers asks.

'Yes, Bratland,' the others confirm.

Sellers chuckles. 'Bratland is as meek as a lamb. You don't need to worry about him. He's just a bit blunt. It's typical of the south-Scandinavian way,' says Sellers.

'I don't know if I want to let a rascal like that anywhere near the Holbein,' says Blaise, gently but honestly.

'Rascal? Ha, no, Bratland is trustworthy. He's the obsessive type. He's been doing music, surfing and other sad activities for years. He might seem a bit irritable, perhaps, but there's not a bad bone in him. He is a bit sceptical, however, about nicer establishments like this,' says Sellers. 'Is that what you've noticed? Once, he was completely floored by a complex, and much too big, gourmet set menu. Bratland couldn't cope with it at all, and completely broke down. The meal arrived far too late in the evening, together with a pre-composed wine selection, a so-called "wine package", replete with red wines of the heaviest sort.

'It led to a night of agonizing visits to the toilet. His ambitions as a gourmand were shelved after that, and Bratland has since borne a grudge towards gourmandism. That's why he might seem a bit harsh towards anything that could be seen as snobbish. Make of that what you will,' concludes Sellers, 'but Bratland likes pre-prepared tacos best of all. He can't get enough of them. Do you have any opinions on the taco as a dish?'

With that, the Maître D' is standing sternly by Anna's side, making sure she packs up her things, her little knapsack, I might have said, because it's a sorry sight. Neither 'bag' nor 'satchel' is a suitable word for describing what Anna is being forced to pack; she's packing her knapsack.

'What on earth is going on?' I ask.

'Time's up,' the Maître D' says.

'Honestly, the girl's father has been held up, and she has to stay until he gets here.'

'One man's floor is another man's ceiling,' the Maître D' says with his big, bloated face close to mine.

'Would you mind putting a lid on the sayings?' I'm flaring up inside. He continues to stare. Anna is standing with her knapsack all packed, looking at us. I notice that her face is slightly pale. There's no doubt she's tired. What do I do now?

'Come and sit with us, Anna.'

It's Child Lady, here she is, circling, getting involved. Why is she butting in? She looks very sincere. But, I think, Child Lady's true face is also a mask, and an awful one.

'We've got space over here!' she says. The Maître D' looks like he's had some kind of stroke.

'And we need our starters and aperitifs!' Sellers shouts. He holds his index finger in the air.

'We're ready for the starters!'

'See?' says Child Lady. 'Old Mr Sellers is here too. He misses you.'

'Come here, my girl,' Sellers says, letting his index finger drop to become a hook which he moves through the air, beckoning to Anna.

'Oi, Moon Boots!' Child Lady says with a gasp. 'There's a seat next to the dashing Mr Blaise.'

'OK,' says Anna. Anna places her knapsack against the chair and greets him and The Pig sweetly and politely with her little hand. Sellers leans across the table in an avuncular fashion and asks her if there was any awkwardness with the Maître D' over there.

'Awkwardness, has there been any awkwardness?' he persists.

'Not really,' says Anna, nobly following this up by saying that she does in fact understand why children aren't allowed to be in here so late.

'No, don't you listen to that blowfish,' Sellers whispers, blowing out his cheeks. Anna giggles. 'We'll get him moving now. Watch this,' he says with a wink. 'Maître D'? Excuse me, Maître D'?'

The Maître D' turns around, full to the brim of stern, Protestant work ethic – the general principle behind the capitalist machinery, as Edgar likes to claim – and nods doggedly. Sellers says that his 'niece' would like to have profiteroles while the adults have their starters. The Maître D' purses his lips slightly as he takes the order.

'Now they're having starters!' the Maître D' says, startled, to the Bar Manager and me. 'How has this happened?'

'Not easy to explain. Sellers turned everything back to front,' I mumble, 'he reversed their dinner. We just have to do it the wrong way round.'

'The girl can stay a while longer, but then that's it,' the Maître D' commands, heading into the kitchen with his work-ethic stride, to pass on the order from table 13 in person.

'Face-lotion time,' the Bar Manager mutters.

Once the starters are ready, the Maître D' serves them himself, making a show of it, simply squeezing me out of the picture. Is this some kind of punishment? He serves the starters which, in reality, have become some kind of dessert: Kalix roe, the famous caviar from Norrbotten, produced by the little vendace fish, to Child Lady. Twelve European flat oysters, or 'kisses from the sea', as Sellers provocatively chose to call them as he ordered, four for each of the men. Blaise looks dumbfounded when the shells are placed in front of him, but he slurps down the first. Anna has been given five choux-pastry balls and some warm chocolate sauce in a metal sugar bowl, which she eats rapidly with the comically long dessert spoon.

Sellers wins her over just as quickly. To include 'the younger generation' in the conversation, he says, pointing to Anna, he wants to have an 'exchange' around the whole concept of streaming, but he repeatedly says 'streamings', something which cheerful little Anna notices. She giggles and bites her lip and waits for The Pig's and Blaise's reactions, and is now completely infatuated with Sellers after just five minutes. She's sold. And, as though that wasn't enough – he's now lighting up a cigarette and brazenly flouting the smoking ban.

'There's a lot that needs streamings,' he says thoughtfully, taking a deep drag. He breathes out a thick column of smoke. A girl of nine can barely have seen how cigarette smoke behaves indoors. Soft and bluish, it rises towards the ceiling.

'Don't take the smoke from the elders,' says Anna.

'Listen to her!' Sellers laughs. '*The Child Wordsmith.* I have faith in you,' he says. And would you believe it, the Maître D' has gone all abstract now: before they finish their oysters, he goes over to ask, would they like a little sparkling wine before their food?

'A glass of prosecco, perhaps, while you wait for your starters? Or champagne, we have the good Ruinart Brut, fresh, creamy.'

Sellers is beaming, as malicious as only a scamp can be.

'Fantastic,' he says, 'some bubbly before the meal. Thank you.'

Blaise knocks back oyster number two and swallows firmly. Is he gulping?

The phrase 'ruddy-faced' fits the Maître D' wonderfully. He's extremely ruddy, a real rud. He pours the Ruinart slowly, very slowly, a textbook example of how to pour sparkling wine, but also completely against the traditional European serving practice. The champagne is only just running out of the neck of the bottle. Like some kind of blood pudding in a suit, he stands there pouring, well within a Maître D's customary behaviour, but also verging on collapse because everything is going backwards. If it had been down to Sellers, the sparkling wine would have trickled back up into the bottle from the glasses.

'There's nothing like the fizz of champagne before food, quaffed down from Marie Antoinette's nipple,' Sellers says ceremoniously, sipping handsomely from his shallow coupe.

Blaise grips his last oyster, but manages to drop it and it falls, with a good spoonful of shallot and muscatel vinegar, on to one of his phenomenal lapels. The mollusc rolls down Blaise's entire left flank and lands on his thigh.

It leaves behind a dark trail, like a snail's. It's a shock to the entire table. Everyone watching, the Bar Manager and myself included, gasps inwardly. You can actually hear the meticulousness break, not to mention Blaise's wallet jingling. Blaise looks at The Pig with an expression of disgust and then jumps up like a coiled spring. The Pig follows him. The Maître D' has frozen in a position resembling a Greek statue, but he composes himself and goes to Blaise's aid. 'Let's go and see old Pedersen in the cloakroom,' he says with vigour. 'Pedersen will have a solution for this, he knows his stuff.' With hurried steps, the three rush out into the foyer, where Pedersen is sitting, full of experience and old tricks.

Child Lady turns to Anna and asks whether she isn't tired.

'You're up late every evening,' she says. Anna shakes her head. 'You're so pretty,' Child Lady continues. Sellers' eyes suddenly freeze, and his boyish smile disappears. He points to Child Lady with his cigarette and says, with extreme force, 'I'll short-circuit you.'

Child Lady, otherwise a machine for creating envy, loses her poise and glances to one side; it's as though she has been emptied. She pauses. Anna's eyes dart back and forth. Sellers looks at me and nods firmly. And, in a rare, clear moment, I spot my chance.

'Come on, Anna,' I say. Anna gets up.

'Grab your bag and wait under the mezzanine. I'll be right back.'

Anna does as she is told, and I run over to the spiral

staircase and rush upwards, making the iron framework creak. Bent over at the top, I see old Johansen sitting with his face pointing straight up and his mouth open. The back of his head is resting on his neck fat, completely still. Is he dead? No, his fingers are moving, he's playing.

'What about playing one of those night-time tunes that Bach wrote for Count Kaiserling,' I say, 'possibly No.21?' Old Johansen straightens up and seamlessly transitions into one of Bach's night tunes.

Anna is standing obediently with her bag on her back. On the short wall beneath the mezzanine, that false ceiling, there is a small wooden door with a bolt. It's the old wood store, or wood chamber, if you like, no longer in use. A blue plaque screwed into place between all the other adornments reads *Annar Andredagen (1942–45)*.

'In here,' I say to Anna, undoing the bolt on the door. 'A man called Annar hid in here every other day during the war, they say,' I tell her. 'Look at all the newspaper cuttings! It's empty now. Pretty good space, eh? We'll lie you down in here, Anna. Dad isn't here yet. It's late. You can look at all the cuttings on the walls here. There's a picture of Andy Panda. I have to keep working my shift.'

'Is your bandage OK?' Anna asks.

'Yes, it's nice and tight. Thanks so much. Now let's make a nest for you in here. Come, Anna. Crawl in.'

I go back to the kitchen. In the wardrobe corner, I grab an armful of waiter's jackets that aren't being used. The Chef moves and makes space for me.

And once we've made a nest with the white waiter's

jackets in the old wood store, and Anna is lying down, with her knapsack as a pillow and a jacket on top to soften it, and we've put the candle from table 19 in the sconce, we hear a gentle knock from outside. The door opens with a creak and Sellers peers in. He smiles.

'Shall I tell you a fairy tale?' he says. Anna nods from her lying position. I try to draw breath but end up gasping rather than inhaling. Then, before I can stop him, Sellers crawls in, sits beside the girl and begins.

'Are you lying there, staring

What is it you're staring at
Do you want a walloping?
Control your eyeballs

Staring
Gawking
There are so many nice things to glare at

It's glowing
Shining
Gleaming

Watch out your eyes don't fall out of your head
Then they fall out

The eyes roll out and over the ground
Into the troll's bag

The troll runs to the hills
Where he hammers the eyes into coins

The troll gets rich, so rich

The troll takes the eyes to the mountain
Inside are all the eyes, and they are coins.'

The Name

Anna lies quietly in her nest. After ten minutes, she begins to breathe more heavily, and a jolt passes through her body. The door to the cubbyhole creaks – I don't want to wake her. Best to sit here a bit longer. When is a child sleeping deeply? I wonder if I should reach out in the darkness and stroke her head, but decide against it. Instead, I quietly, soothingly repeat her name: 'Anna, Anna.'

Sellers has vanished. Is that Blaise I can hear out in the restaurant? The wall distorts the voices, so I don't know who is saying what. It's like I'm blind. I can hear them. People like Blaise and The Pig, they don't give in. People like Sellers. They're tireless. And Child Lady. Always coming back.

'It's a paradox that life is so ordinary when it's so short and unusual,' someone out there mumbles. Who is it? I don't think it's the Maître D'; his maxims are more irritating, less philosophical. Maybe it was The Pig. He's old enough to think like that.

'Fame is a mask that eats away at the face,' someone else says. A woman. There's no way Child Lady could have come out with something so inspired.

Anna stirs. I continue to say her name: 'Anna, Anna.' It's all I can think of. It's my way of rocking the crib, of lulling the girl to sleep. It's a powerful technique. I can feel it working on me, too.

* * *

Everything seems suddenly muffled. Judging by the subdued hum of voices, there are fewer people in the restaurant. Did I nod off? It does seem like I was out of it for a moment. Then I hear the sound of General Manager M. Hill's fingers tapping away at the little adding machine. She's come down to cash up, like she does every evening. She descends the two flights of stairs, wearing an exquisite blouse and with her hair soberly tied up, accompanied as usual by her son, K. Hill, who is now twenty-four years old. They sit in their usual spot, at the little table for two behind the pillar. The son is learning how to cash up the old-fashioned way.

I'm all ears. I know exactly how the sequence goes. The General Manager will be given a glass of Niepoort, just like Widow Knipschild, and this glass will be accompanied by a thin cigarette, a menthol. As a rule, it's me who sets out the glass and the ashtray, one on either side of the calculator, but now I'm here, in this cubbyhole, and it's getting a bit late to come crawling out. Late and strange, to say the least, to come crawling out of the wall. Who'll do the job?

The ashtray is an antique, a small cast-iron hand, out-stretched so that you can tap ash into its waiting palm. Stinking of cigarette butts, it's kept hidden behind one of the terracotta pots next to the mirror (the one that makes us all look fat), just beyond the lavish shelves of booze the Bar Manager oversees. I can hear her now, lifting down bottle after bottle, wiping them and putting them back. Does anyone but me actually know where the General Manager's personal ashtray is kept?

M. Hill keeps all the till receipts from the day to the left of the adding machine, a ledger to the right. She goes through all of the takings meticulously. Her polished nails tap the buttons. Every number is entered, I hear the calculator whirr each time she adds an amount. A long strip of paper appears, the sums printed on it. All the fig-ures, the takings, are crunched. The numbers are then added to the ledger. Her cigarette burns out in the ashtray, not many puffs are taken.

It's like this every night: once M. Hill sits down with the adding machine, it's over. By then, even the slowest guests have settled up, and now they need to get going. They politely take their leave, nodding in the direction of the General Manager. They go over to the cloakroom and pull on their coats, jackets, cloaks. Hats are less common these days, but they do still make an occasional appearance;

Pedersen still has to hand over the odd hat. The Maître D' remains, dotting the 'i's and crossing the 't's, making sure that every last detail is as it should be. Everything has to be reset. He's very particular about that.

* * *

Anna is sleeping now, I should think. I don't move. I'll have to stay put. Through the old air vent above the candle sconce in the dark room, I can see the cinema and, beyond that, the theatre – the meeting places of the past. If I move my head right up against the wall, I can also see the bottom of our sign. Oddly enough, the sign is split into two, with an upper and a lower panel. It stretches from one end of the façade to the other, above the entrance, and is supported by four narrow pillars of bright orange Skyros marble. That's how it has been for years, looming horizontally across the building like some vast European reptile.

Unlike with a church window, which is illuminated from the outside, like an advertisement for the glory to come, there is an opening in the wall at the back of our sign, along its whole length, meaning that every evening, the light from the restaurant shines through the sign and on to the street. The sign functions as a kind of dim light box. Pedersen is in charge of the two ceiling lamps that produce this effect. When he leaves for the night, he turns them off.

On the upper panel, 'The Hills' is written in a pale, almost white script, surrounded by dark slabs of onyx that are framed by a flamboyant pattern in lead. The lower panel is a slanted box, an oversized cabinet, with straight lines of white, blue and red around the name 'The Hills'. The pieces of glass here form a speckled font, with green, yellow and pink elements. The name of the restaurant is repeated, in other words, one on top of the other; we see a duplicate: 'The Hills The Hills'. Some kind of stutter, perhaps.

Acknowledgements

With thanks to:
Gardar, Marie & Lilja
Øyvind Ellenes
Ingeri Engelstad
Niclas Salomonsson
Gardar Eide Einarsson
John Kelsey
Katharine Burton
Leander Djønne
Halvor Rønning
Richard Øiestad
Peter Amdam
Tonya Madsen